"You can taste the ballpark dust, feel the smack of the glove, and feel assured that, somehow, these three strongly drawn characters will push on to victory."

—BOOKLIST

"While ostensibly a contemporary baseball story, Hazelgrove's expansive fifth novel also tackles issues of class, immigration law, and inequity. Thirteen-year-old Ricky Hernandez has a 75 mph pitch and dreams of making the freshman baseball team in Jacksonville, Fla., as the first step toward a professional career. He's dyslexic, of Mexican and Puerto Rican descent, and is ceaselessly taunted by his peers, led by a kid named Eric with an inside track to making the team. While most of Ricky's teammates can afford sports camp and private lessons, he and his mother are broke due to his abusive father's lack of financial support and his mother's mounting medical bills. Despite her deteriorating health, she has loads of attitude, brains, and charm. She singlehandedly persuades their neighbor, "The Pitcher," who played in the World Series, to set aside his beer, leave his garage, and coach Ricky.

Hazelgrove (Rocket Man) measures out a generous sprinkling of American idealism while weaving in legitimate threads of sorrow, employing the oft-used baseball metaphor to fresh and moving effect. Adult characters are particularly well-crafted, giving the book crossover potential."

—PUBLISHERS WEEKLY

"Hazelgrove knits a host of social issues into a difficult but believable tale in which junior high–age Ricky has a gift: He can throw a mean fastball...An engaging, well-written sports story with plenty of human drama—this one is a solid hit."

—KIRKUS

"Hazelgrove is skilled at creating fully fleshed-out characters, and the dialogue carries the story along beautifully. While there is plenty of sports action, *The Pitcher* is ultimately about relationships, and personal growth of the characters will appeal to a wide audience."

—SCHOOL LIBRARY JOURNAL

The Pitcher 2: Seventh Inning Stretch
by William Hazelgrove

© Copyright 2015 William Hazelgrove

ISBN   978-1-63393-002-5

Published by

Café con Leche

an imprint of Köehler Books

3 Griffin Hill Court
The Woodlands, TX 77382
281-465-0119
www.cafeconlechebooks.com

bitlit

A free eBook edition is available
with the purchase of this print book.

CLEARLY PRINT YOUR NAME ABOVE IN UPPER CASE

Instructions to claim your free eBook edition:
1. Download the BitLit app for Android or iOS
2. Write your name in **UPPER CASE** on the line
3. Use the BitLit app to submit a photo
4. Download your eBook to any device

For Kitty, Clay, Callie,
and Careen

THE PITCHER 2

SEVENTH INNING STRETCH

WILLIAM HAZELGROVE

VIRGINIA BEACH
CAPE CHARLES

Never let the fear of striking out keep you
from playing the game.

—BABE RUTH

PREGAME

MOM HAS A DREAM, and it's to see me walk down the aisle with my graduating class. In her dream everyone has on the blue caps and gowns, and the Superintendent is reading out the names, and he finally comes to mine. And then I walk up and he hands me my diploma and my mom screams *"You did it, Ricky!"* That's my mom's dream.

Mine is a little different.

In my dream I am on the mound in Wrigley Field and it's the opening game. It is a beautiful day with the wind blowing off the lake, and the sky pure blue. The stands are full, and I am bringing the ball in and throwing the first pitch. I have just signed with the Chicago Cubs, and I am *The Pitcher*.

What actually happens is somewhere between those two dreams.

1

TY COBB WAS THROWN OUT of baseball for beating up a fan who heckled him. The man had no hands, and Ty Cobb stomped on him with his spikes until the cops pulled him off. When Van Johnson banished him from baseball, his team went on strike in support of him. Cobb went back to playing, and no one remembered who the man was he beat up. Ty Cobb was fined fifty dollars. I would have rather faced Ty Cobb than the wrath of telling someone I wasn't taking her to prom.

Esmeralda's mouth is inhaling French fries and telling me all about her prom dress. And her lips are like blood red and her mouth is white fire with her teeth chomping up and down. I'm nodding and thinking she really is very pretty. She has long dark curly hair, and her earrings jump around like Mom's, and her eyes are deep brown, almost black. We've been dating for like two years. I have known her like all my life because she lives right down the street, and she is already talking about my Major League career and having kids and all sorts of stuff. But right now, the biggest thing she talks about now is prom.

But I have to drop the big one.

"Listen, Es," I begin.

She's doing the head wobble with her mouth moving. The tat of the rose on her shoulder looks blood red, and I have barely made a dent in my quarter pounder because this is not going to be good. She is now slugging on her big Diet Coke that is almost like a bucket of soda, getting her even more wired. There is no good time, so I just lay it out there. Because eventually you just got to pitch, and I figure a curve ball will work here.

But she's babbling on and on, not giving me a chance to deliver.

"And so I told her no way am I getting in a limousine without a bar because if I am going to pay good money...."

Alright, maybe not yet, maybe I should hold off. The truth is I wouldn't even be in this situation if it wasn't for Christine Sanders coming up to me after a Facebook post that MLB scouts were talking to me. Christine is like one of those girls who never talks to Mexican dudes. So, it really freaks me out when she asks if I'm going to prom. I mean, we are talking blond cheerleader, and she is like one of the richest girls in school, with the blue eyes and a cheerleader body. She asks if I will give her a ride home, and we never like even make it to her house.

I mean bam. Right there. I fall in love. And I'm like, Es who? But you know everybody wants to be my friend now, and I ask Christine right then if she wants to go—even though I am going out with Es. And by the time I get home and some of the shock of it all had worn off, I realized that I am going to the prom with *two* girls. And so then I made it my mission to tell Es. But I keep chickening out. So, I decide I got to do it, I got to man-up, right here at McDonald's. She is now draining down more Diet Coke, and I breathe heavy and say again.

"Listen, Es."

"Yeah, you said that," she says.

"Yeah..."

I squirm and my burger is ice cold. I'm getting chicken again, thinking about her temper. She has thrown a few things my way over the years because she gets jealous real easy, and so I know this is not going to over good. But Christine has already gotten her dress, and I'm supposed to go over to her house for dinner, and I figure it is now or never, man, *now or never*.

"Listen, Es."

Her eyes do the mom dance. You know, like angry marbles or something.

"What you think, I'm deaf or something?"

"No," I mutter.

Her eyes really are moms. I mean they shimmy back and forth and light up like pin balls and do the back and forth thing when she is pissed. And right now they are waiting on the dude who is strangling on his words.

"Yeah, listen, Es."

"Rick, you are starting to worry me. Are you getting stoned or something? You already said that three times. "

"Listen, Es."

"Ricky...*what!*"

Alright. So I throw my curve.

I blink and talk down to my burger

"Look, about prom."

"Uh-huh. What about prom?"

"Yeah...."

I kick back and stare out the window and wish I was anywhere else but now. She already bought the dress, bro. *Bought the dress.* But I am going with Christine, who is like some exotic leopard that has slinked into my world, and man, I can't even think when she is around. And like I see this as my future, you know. Exotic women just rolling in when I'm a MLB pitcher.

I throw my pitch.

"Yeah...listen...I...don't think I'm doing the prom thing."

Es is like looking up from her bucket of pop, and her eyes narrow in.

"What did you say?"

I swallow and nod and shake and mumble and grumble and murmur.

"Yeah....I think...I think...I think, Es....I think I'm going to go with Christine."

Smack. My curve was supposed to be in the pitcher's mitt, but I see now it was a lob.

Because the bomb is lit. And Esmeralda's eyes go wide like portals to a very dark universe. Her chewing stops and her fires go cold and her bucket of pop is like right beneath her. Her mouth is slightly open, and I can see where her lipstick has painted her front teeth.

"What did you say?"

I open my mouth.

I mean, I could bail. I could say I was just kidding. I could say anything, but she is leaning in like with her chin slightly above the table and her eyes are doing the mom thing. Side to side. Back and forth, back and forth, back and forth. And now comes ghetto land. She sits straight up. Her chin is going back and forth and her head is wobbling and her mouth is cranking up like an engine.

"Did you just say you are taking somebody else?"

Like she yelled it, but she didn't yell. Sort of like someone loading a gun. I sit up and face her and her head won't stop moving and still I consider turning back. I consider that this might not be such a good idea after all, and maybe I should just tell Christine I am already committed. But this is not what I want to do, so I just say like a dumbass.

"Yeah."

Then her mouth rotates once, and her eyes pin me to the booth.

"Christine? Christine who?"

"Oh..."

"She's a cheerleader," I say.

And now, man. I don't know how many liters McDonald's puts in a large Diet Coke, but I can tell you this, it is enough to take a shower. I mean, she grabbed up that Diet Coke so fast it was like I never saw it coming, and all of a sudden the world goes dark and fizzy and ice and pop flow all down through my shirt and through my underwear and down into my pants. And by the time I open my eyes, Es is up in the middle of the McDonald's with everyone staring at us.

Es is dropping F-bombs like every other word. Then she calms—just a little.

"After I bought my dress, you are taking somebody else!"

And her head is bobbing and her mouth is moving and she's got her hands on her hips, and she is crying. That is the worst part, and now here comes my ring, which hits me in the forehead. And now here comes my letter jacket, which slaps me in the face. Now comes the bracelet I gave her, which puts a welt on the right side of head, and now her spikes are up and doing some real damage to my knees. Now here comes my burger, which bounces off my nose and leaves ketchup on my cheeks. Fries rain down from above, and then my own Coke goes into my eyes and I'm blind again and I can feel someone slapping me and kicking me and crying, and then all of a sudden she is gone, man.

And I open my eyes, and the whole McDonald's is staring at the dude covered in pop, ketchup, fries, meat, pickles with welts on his face and bruises on his knees, and I smile back and say,

"We aren't going to prom."

And then some old man with a Marlins cap on who watched the whole thing go down says.

"No shit."

2

FRED SNODGRASS DROPPED THE ball in the 1912 World Series. He played for New York and he was in left field and the ball was a straight up fly, and Snodgrass got under it and then just dropped it. Boston went on to win. For the rest of his life Fred Snodgrass was haunted by that moment. Everyone remembered him as the man who lost the 1912 World Series. Sitting with Mom in front of the man from the Immigration Department, I felt like she was Fred Snodgrass and would never live down the fact she had come to America illegally.

Like Fred Snodgrass. They just wouldn't let her forget.

"What I'm saying, Mrs. Hernandez, is you have to show us why you should be allowed to stay in the United States."

"I am married to him," Mom says, showing her wedding ring from the Pitcher. "He's American, and I am his wife."

"Well, I am afraid there's some question about your motivations."

That's how this dude in the tie and blue suit with the perfect haircut said it. We are in our living room. This dude's dark blue car with the stubby antenna with the star on the license plate is parked in our driveway. And Mom is looking at him like she wants to vaporize him, and the Pitcher looks like he wants to take his head off with a bat. "This is all bullshit!'

That's Mom. Curly dark hair with eyes blazing and her mouth pinched and her fist in the air. You remember her temper, but in this case she is right. Three years of lawyers and money, and she still isn't a citizen yet. And now this guy appears, and he looks like all he wants to do is deport Mexicans. Mom is standing over the guy like she is going to take him out.

"A Mrs. Payne provided us with quite a file...." He looked up, his eyes almost friendly. "Did you do something to her? I have never seen someone so obsessed with the legal status of someone else."

Mom's eyes flatten with her gum moving a million miles a minute. Yeah, can you believe it? Eric's mom. Like the dark force has come back. Darth Vader of the baseball moms. You would think after all this time she would get over it, but not the Paynes. Eric now plays in the outfield, and I think that just burns her that I have been the starting high school Pitcher for the last three years, and I have been kicking ass.

Mom stares at Mr. Government.

"Yeah. My son beat her son out to be pitcher of the high school baseball team," she says.

Mr. Government just stares at her and smiles. Then he laughs shortly and makes the ticking noise. Talk about a nerd. He had to be one of those dudes with pencils and pens always in his pocket in high school.

"You're kidding," he says.

"No." Mom shakes her head. "She's a bitch."

His eyebrows go up, and then he goes into this nodding thing as if he is saying *I see, a bitch*. But he then clears his throat, and the Pitcher, my stepdad, is staring at him like he wants to take his head off with a Louisville Slugger. He has been quiet up until now, but I can tell he is pissed. The vein on the right side of his forehead has inflated like a snake.

"She is a bitch, and it's bullshit you would let her manipulate you like this. My wife deserves to be a citizen. She is more American than that rock head woman will ever be."

Yeah to the Pitcher; I know he wants a cigarette. He is sitting there with his hawk eyes and his hair combed back, which has more grey in it now, but his hands are still steady and he looks like he could take Mr. Government apart piece by piece.

"Hmmm...." The man says then squints down at his paper. "Well, she has painted quite a picture...." He holds up this fat file. "She contends you only married Mr. Langford so your son could try out for the high school baseball team, and that the marriage is a sham so you could stay in the country."

"What a load of crap," the Pitcher rumbles in his plaid shorts and yellow golf shirt. "That woman's head is full of rocks. "

"She's a bitch," I say.

"Ricky," Mom says.

"You just said it," I point out.

"That's different," she says.

The government man shakes his head.

"Yes. Well. The problem is we only have Mrs. Payne's side of the story, and she has provided us with documentation, affidavits. She also says you married Mr. Langford for his money."

"Well, she screwed up there," the Pitcher mutters.

"She's nuts," I say.

Mom is staring at the man like she can't believe what he is saying. It's like three years have just vanished, and we are right back to where we started, only I made the team. But that darkness is back, like something outside the door that you just don't want to let it. She shakes her head, and her eyes are doing the death dance. She stands up and looks down at the little man.

"Is that all, Mr. Jones?'

Really? The dude's name is Mr. Jones. How white can you get? He shrugs and raises his eyebrows and starts putting the papers back in his black briefcase. He reminds me of a hen the way he is clucking and folding papers, and then he stands up and adjusts his glasses and faces Mom.

"I suppose so; basically, you have two weeks to present to me the other side. A story if you will of your life now that will refute Mrs. Payne's contentions and allow the Department of Immigration to settle your case once and for all.'

Yeah. The Department of Immigration. No immigration reform here man. What happened to Obama's plan and pathways to citizenship, and all that crap? They are just busy getting people back to Mexico, and this dude is like something from the Matrix.

You know the agents. *Mr. Anderson.* Mom has on a skirt and high heels and a white blouse with her dangling earrings. She fires back.

"What, you want me to explain it to you?"

Mr. Jones shakes his head and laughs lightly.

"No, no. I prefer a written report. Just tell me the story of your life and your family and give me a picture of your day-to-day," he says like he's giving us an award or something.

Mom mouths day to day and shakes her head.

"Ricky you will have to write it," she says almost to her herself.

I shrug.

"Yeah. No problem, Mom."

I have been burning it down in English, and my teacher Mrs. Shanny says I should write more because I have a real talent. I don't know. I just write the way I talk, and that's not hard, because, as you know, I like to talk. So, Mr. Jones picks up his briefcase all shiny and black. And I know what is coming. He had kept looking at the pictures in our living room of the Pitcher winning the series. Mom said the pictures in the garage should be in the living room because they will get moldy. So she put them in different rooms, but the one of the Pitcher jumping into his catcher's arms is in our living room. And Mr. Jones can't keep his eyes off it.

He shakes his head, and looks at the Pitcher.

"So, you really pitched in a World Series?"

The Pitcher looks at him with these dull eyes, then nods slowly.

"Yeah, and you really work for the government?'

Mr. Jones mouth gets all tight and flat.

"You people have a good day."

Mom pulls open the door for him and Mr. Jones leaves. I watch his car go back down the drive. Some of the neighbors watch, too. You don't want dudes like that in your drive. Mom and the Pitcher are now sitting on the couch, and they are holding hands like someone just died. I guess someone did if a dream is a *someone.* Two weeks. We got two weeks to come up with a story that will allow mom to stay in the country.

And I have to write it.

Our day to day, huh? Yeah. Right. Well. Here it comes.

3

THE FIRST TIME I SAW Bailey Cruise was in March when we were playing an exhibition game against a high school from the other side of town. I had heard about some kid from Texas who was pitching almost a hundred miles an hour. The rap was he was with his family in an apartment but were moving across town to our school district when their house was ready. Right now he was playing for East, which is our rival school.

It is the bottom of the third, and I have been the starting pitcher on South High Varsity now for two years, and things are going really well. I have a lot on my mind, because midterms just proved what I knew all along that my grades were not so good. The scouts have been hovering like flies. I mean, some smaller college scouts, but MLB scouts, too. The Pitcher says don't get a big head and that those rock heads don't know shit from Shinola about baseball. Still, they want to come by the house and have a meeting.

The Pitcher says that we will see what they have to say. Mom says no way. She says I am going to college because it might not work. I might get hurt, or maybe I'll lose my ability to pitch, or maybe I might not like it. Then what? Where will I be then without a college degree? She's talking about a *Moneyball* scenario. You know, the movie with the Billy Beane deal where he gets drafted and then just can't perform. It happens. Guys who are outstanding in high school hit the Majors, and for whatever reason, they just don't have it. Like the one coach in the movie says, "We are told at some point we can't play the children's game anymore...we just don't know when it's going to happen."

And then they slide the check across the table. That is the part I like. Slide that check over, man.

The Pitcher points out to Mom that he never had a degree and things worked out okay. Mom looks at him with her eyes blazing, you know the look, and says, "I rest my case." And then stomps out of the garage. I mean, the Pitcher didn't end up so bad, you know. MLB twenty-five years, and then a house in Florida with a big screen in the garage. I watch that television almost as much as he does. I mean, I'm seventeen now, and we both spit Skoal into a coffee can and even pop a few Good Times together. Don't tell your mother, he says, and I don't. She would serve me up, man, if she knew I was popping beers and dipping Skoal, but the garage is our man cave.

So it's the third inning, and this dude with this blue helmet with orange flames on the side steps up. He is about my size, which is now just under six foot. Growth spurt. Just one day. *Pow,* and I grow like six inches. I'm tall and lanky and I even beefed up some after pumping iron with Jimmy one summer. I had to be cool not to screw up my arm. I have a goatee that The Pitcher says looks really stupid and Mom said looks cute. I almost cut it off when she said that, but all the Majors League pitchers are growing beards, so I got to have something. Still keep the hair short though, because it's gotten even hotter in Florida, if you can believe that.

So I am staring at this guy with the flaming blue sparkly helmet, and his eyes are like the same color as Eric's. They are like blue diamonds, and with his blond hair and his jaw working out on some gum, he does not look like he is from anywhere around here. I figure I'll give him a brush back and then a fastball low and inside, and then finish him with, you guessed it, my changeup.

He turns around and says something to the ump, and that's when I see his name on the back of the helmet. BAILEY. Come on! What a hotdog, man. I'm amazed the coach even allowed that helmet in the park. It was like a walking advertisement for this guy. So I'm kind of grinning on the mound and look at Coach Hoskins, who shrugs and makes this motion with his hand, which means fastball. I'm going to show BAILEY who is boss.

So I pick a spot right by his chin. Like the Pitcher says, you gotta have a spot. So I go into my windup and let fly. I'm real smooth now. Like a well-oiled machine. It's all muscle memory. How fast do I pitch? Ninety-five miles an hour is my best, but I am only getting faster, and I put a lot of heat on this one. Mr. Helmet leans his head back as the ball nips inside. I don't get the call, but I figure I have unnerved him.

"Ball!"

Bailey doesn't seem too impressed though. He just keeps chewing his gum and hits the plate with his bat a few times and then crouches back down like he's A-Rod or something. I take the ball back, and it's a beautiful day in May for Florida. Not too hot with the sand blowing around in the infield, and I'm looking at these two dudes in the stands who don't look like college scouts. They are in khaki pants with those golf shirts, and they have matching Ray Bans like the Blues Brothers or something. They got MLB written all over them with the little Polo dude on their shirts.

So it really is my time to smoke the guy with the flaming helmet and put out his fire. I'm bringing the heat now. Right now, it is time to let Mr. Bailey know who the man is.

I bring in the ball and tilt my hat down low. This is my signal to my team. Juan is like giving me the signal, and I shake off a sinker and he knows where I am going. We know each other now, man, after like a hundred games. It's like we are one person, and he settles back and waits.

And just like before, I take my breath. You know, get in the zone. I can hear the wind and the people in the stands and the other team talking trash. *Come on, Bailey. Do it, Bailey. You the man, Bailey.* Bailey is about to get rocked. I look down from the mound and meet his eyes with his jaw still moving and his bat hovering like an angry bee. Time to go home, Bailey.

I kick in to my windup and bring my arm over and whipsaw the ball down toward home plate, and I know it is going to nip ninety-five. And it is like I am gone for a moment. That is how it is with me. When I hit the zone I am somewhere else, and that is when I hear the crack. A fastball meeting a bat sounds like a rifle shot, and now I am moving my neck and watching that ball go flying straight up and over the back centerfield back fence.

I am turned around, which is really bad for a pitcher, and stare at that white pill against the blue curtain. Like a Babe Ruth kind of homerun where it just keeps going. My mouth is wagging, and I just stare. You don't want to be facing the back fence, ever. And now I watch those flames round first and second, then third and then head for home. And here is the thing. This guy is booking! You would never know he hit a homerun. He is running like the ball is right behind him, and those orange flames are a blur as he slides into home and then pops up. It was like some kind of demonstration of how the perfect baseball player should run.

I watch Bailey dust himself off, and he looks over then and grins at me right before he hits all those high fives coming at him. It's like he said, there is a new sheriff in town. And I feel like Billy Beane, and I am hearing that dude again in *Moneyball* except this time he is speaking to me. *You never know when we are going to be told when you can't play the children's game. But we are all told at some point.*

And I watch that sparkly blue flaming helmet float all the way back to the bench. I vowed then to put out those flames any way I can, because this fire could burn down the house I have been working on for three years. And here's the thing.

It got worse.

4

NOW BAILEY IS ON the mound, and those fire bolts are throwing fastballs like flaming meteorites. Like in *The Natural* where Roy Hobbs gets shot in Chicago and he disappears and then surfaces ten years later, and everyone is like, where did this dude come from and nobody knows. I can't understand where a guy with an arm like this has been hiding for the last ten years. And that's how I feel watching Bailey Cruise on the pitcher's mound. Where the hell did this guy come from? I'll tell you. Texas. Bailey Cruise is his name, and he just moved in from Texas. It's like he is Roy Hobbs. Everyone just stands around with their mouth open, watching him warm up. The ball explodes the catcher's mitt. *Pow!* Then again, and again.

It looks like he is pitching a hundred miles an hour.

No. Not one hundred, but ninety-two Then ninety-three. Then ninety-four.

The Pitcher is by the fence, and I walk over to him, and he doesn't say a thing. He just squints and drops the cigarette below him and stubs it with his tennis shoe.

"Can you believe this guy?" I say.

"I believe he is fast and can hit," he says.

I turn and make this noise with my mouth hanging open like someone just slipped a joker into a deck of cards.

"Nice helmet," the Pitcher says, spitting into the dirt.

"That is ridiculous. Did you see those stupid fire bolts?"

The Pitcher nods slowly.

"Yeah. And you did, too. That's why they are there."

I stare at him.

"What do you mean?'

The Pitcher shrugs.

"He wants you to be staring at those fire bolts while he belts your changeup out of the park. Then you're playing his game and not your own."

He was right, of course, and I was fixated on that sparkly blue flaming helmet.

"Yeah, I know," I mutter.

"You told him what you were going do," he says, staring at Bailey on the mound. "You telegraphed your delivery the whole way. He's no fool, and he figured after that brush-back you'd give him something, and you did."

I stare at the Pitcher. Like I said, his hair is almost white now. I mean, he is still big and smokes like a hundred cigarettes a day and drinks Good Times, but he limits himself to three a day after Mom made him go to the AA meetings. He spits into the dust again.

"One thing is for sure. You can't give a guy like that a straight fast ball."

I turn and watch Bailey wind up, and I see a tat up on his right arm. Mom laid down the law a while ago. *No tats!* The Pitcher has tats, but his are just blue blobs now. He told me to go to the pool and look at all the fat guys with tattoos. He said only pitchers with no talent get tats. I pointed out that a lot of MLB pitchers have tats. "Like I said, only the guys without talents get tats," he finished.

But Bailey Cruise has a tat, and stud in his right ear. To me he looks all MLB, man.

"Just don't let him get under you with that fastball," the Pitcher says walking back to sit by Mom.

"Yeah," I mutter.

So it gets bad real fast. Bailey knocks off our two leadoff

guys like they never saw a fastball in their life. One. Two. Three. You're out. I mean, I would like to say he was moving it around and pinching the corners, but they looked like straight fastballs to me. The worst thing is this Bailey guy doesn't do any of the usual hotdog stuff you see when pitchers nail down the fastballs. He's like a machine. He just takes the ball from the catch and lets fly again.

Coach Hoskins walks up to me, and I can see in his eyes that he's thinking what I am thinking. Something along the lines of what the F.... Mom says I still can't use the F-bomb, and I said I am almost eighteen and everybody uses it now. "Not around me, they don't, carbron," she says. And she is right about that. So no F-word, but maybe one day.

"Don't overthink that fast ball. The guys are jumping the gun. Let it come to you," Coach says, but he looks worried. I mean, I look worried, too.

"How fast you think it's coming, Coach?'

Coach Hoskins, who has gotten even bigger in the last few years, raises his hands like a man who has just seen an alien or something. He has this brown hair with snow at his temples and these recessed blue eyes that are like hidden behind Ray-Bans twenty-four seven. He shakes his head slowly.

"I don't know...fastest I've seen," he says.

This does not give me confidence. I look over, and the two MLB guys are standing by the fence with their eyes glued on Bailey Cruise. This has disaster written all over it, and I try and not think that way, which I call the *old way*. The *new way* is that everything will work out and go my way. The old way, like back when I was trying to make the high school team, was that nothing will work out and things are only going to get worse. It's sort of like this black cloud that follows me around, and most of the time it's so far away I can barely see it. But now I see that cloud, and it is getting bigger.

"C'mon, Ricky, you can do it!"

I look over, and my spirits lift. That's Christine. She is definitely part of the new way. We have been dating for almost a year. She is over by the stands with her girls in my South jacket with her long blond hair and blue eyes, and like I said, she is like something that came when the word got around that MLB scouts were interested in me. I didn't say anything, but you know how Facebook is, man. One person says it, and, *wham*, everybody knows. So like suddenly people who never talked to me before are now my friends, and Christine is now dating yours truly.

"Show that asshole who is boss, Ricky!"

That's Jimmy. He is like part of the old way. He is over in his hoody by the stands with some girls with their long black hair flowing back in the wind with pumps and hoop earrings and nose-pins and super red lips and black fingernails. Mexican chicks, you know. Christine is staring at me and gives me a thumbs-up, and she is all down with being the wife of a Major League pitcher. We talk about it all the time and get real excited, but like now she is staring at me with the same sort of what-the-F stare, you know. Like I say, this gum-chomping blue-eyed creature whipping one hundred mile an hour fastballs is all Roy Hobbs, and like I sure wish he would go back to Texas and take his sparkly helmet with the flames with him.

Because I am up and looking toward the pitcher's mound, and those weird blue eyes now look like Eric's. And that is something I hoped I would never see again.

5

BALLPARKS DETERMINE WHO A city is. When the Federal League was formed, they gave players the right to free agency. Up until then, everyone was stuck with the reserve clause, which meant a team owned you. The Federal League also gave Chicago Wrigley Field. The Federal League didn't last, but Wrigley Field did. It's like from something new came something old. Bailey was like that. Something new that I associated with something old.

Like the first bad thing you know in a long time. Ever since I made the high school team and the Pitcher married Mom, we had been cruising along. The *new way* was everywhere. Mom was happy and the Pitcher was happy, and we hung in the garage together and watched ball games, or we went and caught the Marlins. We went to Cooperstown once to check out the Hall of Fame, and sometimes in the airport we would be sitting there and someone would come up to the Pitcher.

"Hey, aren't you Jack Langford?'

And the Pitcher, he would just sit there and look up and nod. "Yeah."

"Can I have your autograph? I saw that game where you smoked Jim Rice."

And he would sign autographs for the guy or his kids or his grandkids. He never said much about it, just went back to reading the paper or talking to Mom. I thought it was pretty cool. It's like he was branded for life, you know. Like whatever he did, people knew he had pitched a World Series game and had been in the Majors for twenty-five years. Even the guys who took our trash every Tuesday called out. "Hey, Mr. Langford, how's the pitching going?"

In a way he was world famous even though I lived with him now.

Or he would get a call for these fantasy camps where he would go and speak to all these guys who paid thousands of dollars to wear a Detroit Tiger uniform and run the bases and basically be Jack Langford for a weekend. And when he spoke, he talked the same way he does when he tells me how to pitch. "Those rock-heads don't know what they are doing...." But he could have said anything to these guys, because they just hung on every word. And then they would pay him like five grand or something, and the Pitcher would come back home and go sit in his La-Z-Boy with Shortstop and watch ballgames and smoke and drink and spit Skoal.

That dog, man, he loved The Pitcher. He had grayed now, which is something I didn't think dogs did. But his snout is all white now, and he moves a lot slower. The Pitcher said his hips were bugging him, and he gave him Glucosamine and fish oil with his dog food. He said if it worked for humans, it should work for dogs. He put Good Times beer in his water sometimes, and Shortstop would sleep all day and get up and you could tell from his face he was hungover.

The colleges started calling and leaving messages about coming to their school. So we went to a bunch of colleges, and they treated me like I had played in the MLB or something. They talked full-rides and showed me their training facilities, and we went to dinner with the coaches, who just about fell over when they found out Jack Langford was my dad. They stared at him like he was a God and treated me almost the same. Mom would always quiz me after the college visit and ask if I could see myself going there, and I would shrug and say yeah. But I mean, my grades weren't the greatest, Cs mostly. So I was amazed they wanted me. But it was all about baseball really and those ninety-mile-an-hour pitches.

But Mom was not budging.

"You have to get an education, Ricky, in case you can't play baseball."

That was how Mom saw it. But I couldn't imagine not playing, you know. I mean, the Pitcher is a pitcher for life, even though he doesn't play anymore. It's like it's who I am. I am not Ricky who wants to pitch in the MLB. I am a pitcher who wants to play in the Majors. Like a writer is a writer, or a painter is a painter. You just can't help it, because it is who you are. I tried to explain that to Mom a couple times, but I think she saw it like a switch that could be turned on and off.

"You still need an education even if you play in the Majors," is how she saw it.

The Pitcher didn't say anything about college. He never went, and Mom said it was different then. He said it was different then, but he didn't say I should go to college. He just said keep working on my pitching and don't drink my own Kool-Aid. In other words, don't believe any of the press. Don't believe the college guys who tell me how great I am and how they want me to be their star pitcher. He said don't believe in anyone but myself.

And I am trying to do that now standing up at the plate, facing this maniac with the weird blue eyes. I hold the bat ready to smash the bean and can hear the wind in the trees and smell a hotdog and the scent of the grass from the infield. Dust is dancing up in these small circles to the left of the plate, and I am crouching and waiting for it. Bailey is pulling in, and we are two gunslingers facing off in the Old West.

"Knock the shit out of it, Ricky! This guy can't f-ing pitch! '"

That voice is from my nightmares that come when I wake up in a cold sweat and can't get back to sleep. That voice belongs to the darkest days of the old way. I thought that voice had left for good, but now it was right there somewhere in right field. And I looked, which you never do when you are up to bat. You never look away from the pitcher, but I just had to. And I don't see anyone. No one. And I look right back at Bailey, who is drawing back.

"Hit the mother, Ricky!"

I open my eyes and feel electricity jangle right down my spine. It's like someone hit me with a jolt of electricity because I know that voice. I do. It is burned in my brain, and there is only one person I know who would say something like that. Fernando. And it is in that moment when my eyes shoot to right field again. Bailey Cruise lets fly and that ball whizzes right past me, and I hear it smack the catcher's mitt like a rifle shot.

"Strike!"

It's like I had blinked, and Bailey knew just when to shoot that fastball across the plate. Because I had blinked, and when I opened my eyes, Fernando is there by the fence like he never left. He has on his dark glasses and a long ponytail and his big arms with tats rolling all the way up. He has a full goatee with his wallet chain dangling in the sun like a dangerous snake. And his hands are high up on the fence like he is going to climb over it any minute.

Hell has returned.

"Get that mother-f, Ricky!"

I can't believe it. Three years and not a word, and now he is there. My mouth is open, and for a moment I have forgotten where I am. But then I see the two MLB guys who are standing with their arms crossed, and I try and put Fernando out of my head, which is impossible by the way. Why would he come back now? And then I know the answer. You know the answer. The dude comes back for the chips, right. He probably heard that people in the Majors were interested in me, and Fernando has come back for his cut of the pie. Why else would he be at my game?

I move the bat around and wonder if Mom has seen him. I mean it's like the black plague has returned or something. Fernando is all old way and belongs to those really dark times when we thought we were going to lose our home and Mom didn't have health insurance and the Pitcher was just this asshole who lived across the street in his garage and Fernando was this dude coming to steal our money and beat the crap out of Mom. He is staring at me with his dark glasses and hands snaking through the fence.

So I glance over to the stands, and, yeah, Mom has seen him. She is standing up and staring directly at Fernando like some kind of zombie who has just risen from the dead. Fernando is like those dudes in the *Hunger Games,* and he is going to eat everybody. But I have to get my head back. This is not the time to be thinking about Fernando. *Okay. Concentrate. Concentrate.* I am now eying Bailey and crouching and getting ready to meet that fastball on own terms. *Okay, one strike. No big thing. Time to knock it out of the park.*

So what the hell was Fernando doing at my game?

"Strike!"

Didn't even see it. My head was somewhere else, and you can get away with that sometimes. But with this guy, no way. I look over at Coach Hoskins, who is by the dugout with this perplexed look. Why wasn't I even swinging? That ball just slipped by in the breath between seconds. I heard it, but I didn't see it. It was moving that fast.

"Don't take any shit off this guy, Ricky! This guy can't pitch worth shit!"

Vintage Fernando, man. This guy could pitch worth shit. He could pitch more than shit, and if I didn't blot out Fernando like now, I was going down. I moved the bat on my shoulder and reset myself and doubled down staring at Bailey, who was pulling the ball in for his windup. I can feel the buzz of the zone, and I can tell what he is up to now. He is going inside. Just the quiet now. Just the moment.

"Kick his ass, Ricky!"

I blot out Fernando. But that voice is not stopping now. It has come back, and it really doesn't matter why because when the darkness comes, man, it just comes. And then it is night, and you are back in hell and who cares why or how it happened. You just know you are back in the bad place, and all you want to do is get out of it. That is the way it is with any sport, man. It is all attitude. I am the best because I know I am the best. You fulfill your own prophecy, right? Sort of like surfing on a wave and staying up and out of that dark green water right beneath you.

"Kick his f-ing ass, Ricky!

So I fight hard, man. I am Ricky Hernandez, man. I am *the man.* I have a .360 batting average. I routinely hit homers. I make mincemeat out of pitchers, and then I destroy batters. I am the best that has ever come out of South High. I have colleges telling me I don't have to pay a dime and hinting they will give me a car and I will live like a king in the nicest dorms. I have Major League Baseball scouts calling my home and wanting to meet. I see that scene all the time in *Moneyball* where they slide the check across the table. "This is what we think of Ricky and this expresses our confidence in him." I am happening. I am the man.

So bring it on!

"Kick him in the balls, Ricky, with a line drive, man!"

What?

Bailey lets fly and I see that ball and then I don't and I swing with everything I have.

"Strike!"

I have just been struck out by a guy named Bailey Cruise from Texas. And those MLB scouts are walking to the other side of the field to talk to the guy who just smoked the best player ever to come out of South High School. And Fernando comes in for cleanup.

"Tough shit, Ricky!"

6

A-ROD. MARK MCQUIRE. Bailey Hutchinson. They all are like something from another planet. A-Rod and Mark McQuire probably juiced, you know. Well, they did. Steroidal, man. And still they are among the greatest players that ever lived. And I would like to say Bailey juiced man. You know, that would account for his fastball or the way he knocked my fast ball out of the park like it was nothing. But he is not about steroids. He is about like backwoods talent. Something like Mickey Mantle coming out of the fields of Oklahoma and getting in that scout's Cadillac at seventeen and never being the same after that, because real talent has its own clock.

And I am thinking all this while watching Fernando walking to the fence, and I am shocked because his hair has grey streaks and his goatee has snow. The dude walks up to the fence like it's just another day, and I am putting my bat into bat bag and trying to act like I don't see him, but that is impossible because you don't not see a guy like Fernando.

"Hey, Bro!" He calls.

I look up, and he is like a foot away, clinging to the fence like it is a prison. His fat fingers are ink stained with SATAN across his knuckles. Prison did wonders for him. His teeth are almost black, and he walks with a limp, which came from the Pitcher taking him out that day three years ago.

"Whassup," I say.

He comes over and gives me shake and then the hug, and the liquor is like gasoline. You can smell it all over him. He palms a cigarette and cups his lighter, puffing out smoke like some old broken down train engine.

"How you been, man?'

I shrug and feel hot. I am sweating, and it is not that hot. It is just my heart has gone into overtime, and I feel like I am thirteen again with all that old fear. You never knew when Fernando was going to appear and rock your world. He would just show up and create hell and then disappear. So I am in like flight- or-fight mode as I repack my mitt and keep my eyes on my bag and shrug again.

"Alright."

Fernando rubs his arms that are not all that muscular anymore. Kind of fat. And that is because he is kind of fat, and his tats have faded, and his sunglasses are those cheap round kind you get in a gas station. He nods slowly.

"Yeah, man. I did a little stretch, you know, and that's why I haven't been to see you."

Prison. A little stretch. Prison. That's why he hasn't been to see me. My question is why did they let this dude out? Are they that overcrowded? I mean, if there is one guy who should be in prison, it's Fernando. There is no rehabilitation here. Just bad getting worse.

"That's cool," I mutter.

"You and your mom are doing alright, huh? I hear you got MLB scouts looking at you."

"Some."

Gotta love *Facebook,* right? You got a secret you don't want, then put it on *Facebook* and the whole world will know about it, and some dude in prison will read it and get out and head straight for Florida where he can shake down his son he used to beat all the time. Yeah. Social Media is like the cons' friend. Fernando is nodding slowly like he's got all the answers and he is who the scouts want to talk to.

"Yeah, man. That's cool. You be set then, bro. Good thing I taught you early, huh?"

I stare at him, and now my ears are burning man because I know his play. He sees the past a whole different way now. He was the dad who taught me how to play ball, and now he's come for his payoff. It makes me kind of sick, and I am starting to shake.

"Yeah, I was telling my homies that my boy, he is going to be pitching for the Majors and that he won't forget his old man who taught him to pitch, man. I mean, you and me is flesh and blood, bro. You know? I mean, I may have not been around, and I know you won't forget your old man now that you are going to be a millionaire."

"What the f—are you doing here, Fernando?"

That is Mom. She and the Pitcher have walked up behind us, and now Mom is right in his face and he is doing this slow smile.

"Hey, baby. You are looking really good. Married life agrees with you, huh. "

Mom jabs her finger through the air with the Pitcher staring at him like he wants to split his knee again. Mom is like on fire and pushing him back.

"Stay away from Ricky! I don't want you bringing your shit near him, Fernando! What are you even coming around for? No one wants you here. Get out of here before I call the cops!"

He spreads his arms and grins, and I feel the world tilting because the Pitcher has stepped up. Fernando slouches and lifts his right hand.

"What, you going to hit me with a bat again, old man?"

The Pitcher nods slowly.

"Yeah. That's not a bad idea."

"Uh-huh. I got a permanent limp because of your motherf-bat, and one day I'm going to give you some payback. Don't you worry about that, bro...it's coming."

The Pitcher looks down at him and nods cool like this is no big deal. Fernando on the other hand has his arms wide like a gunslinger about to draw. It wouldn't surprise me if he is packing.

"Anytime, rock-head."

Mom pushes Fernando back and screams.

"Get the hell out of here!"

Fernando nods in the old way. He grins slowly, showing all those rotten teeth.

"Wow, still fiery. I forgot that about you, Maria. Bet you still wild, too."

The Pitcher steps forward and Fernando pulls back his leather coat, and no one moves because the hard black metal butt of a gun is hanging out of his low riders. He nods and gestures to the Pitcher.

"You see this? Come any closer, and I'm going to blow your head off."

I can see the black bulge of the gun pushing against his belt. The Pitcher stares at him and spits in the dust at Fernando's feet.

"You don't have the guts, rock-head."

I mean, my heart is like going a million miles a minute and Mom's eyes are big, and Fernando is sweating these fat pearls all over his forehead.

"Try me, old man," he says.

Mom steps back, and I can see she knows he would shoot the Pitcher. So do I. He is that bad.

"What do you want, Fernando?" she asks.

He lets his jacket drop and nods.

"I have come for my due, baby."

Mom is staring at him with her eyes going back and forth.

"What are you talking about?'

Fernando raises his flabby arms and shrugs.

"I mean MLB. And I am his father. And I deserve some payoff, baby, for my part in raising a Major League pitcher."

Mom just stares at him the way I am staring at him. It is like you cannot believe what he is saying. I mean, here is this guy who has like come back from the dead with a gun and it's like a nightmare. I thought people were supposed to have changed who go to prison. You know, reformed and all that. Not Fernando. He came out even worse.

Mom steps up close, and I can see the difference now. It is like the new way and the old way together. Mom has on some nice shorts and a blouse and the big diamond the Pitcher gave her when they got married, and her hair is pinned back and she just looks good, you know. But there is Fernando with his gut

and his cutoff shirt and his grease hair and his low rider pants
and boots and his gun, and they look like two people who should
not know each other. It's like the past meeting the present.

Mom raises her finger. She has guts, man, because that gun
is still right there. She pushes him back.

"You stay away from my son, Fernando. You come close to
him, and I use that gun on your sorry ass. You never did anything
for him, and you will never ever get one red cent from his career.
I will make sure of that!"

But Fernando just shrugs and smiles real evil.

"Oh, you think you a high-society bitch now. That's cool. But
I'm back and I want my due, man. And I will get it one way or
another. He ain't going to leave me behind, man, because I'm
his father."

And I just boil over. I don't even know that I am shouting,
but I am.

"No, you're not! You're some piece of trash that just blew in
because you got nothing else!"

Fernando then looks at me and acts like I didn't say anything.

"Hey, man. You take it easy. Protect that arm, bro. That's our
million-dollar ticket, you know."

He looks at the Pitcher then and nods, tapping his belt.

"I will deal with you later, man."

"Anytime, rock-head."

And then he just goes back to his Harley and kicks it up.
And Mom and I stare at him as he rumbles out of the parking
lot. Mom looks like the old way. Like the bad stuff is back. I
know what she is thinking, man, because for the first time I am
wondering if you can ever really get out. Like you just crawled
out of this dark hole, and now something is pulling you back
in. And that something rides a Harley. The Pitcher walks up
behind Mom, and she doesn't even turn. She is still watching
the road where Fernando rumbled out of site like she expects
him to return

"I thought he was in prison."

Mom turns around, and her eyes are burning bright. "They
let the asshole out."

7

GROVER CLEVELAND WAS ONE of the best pitchers who ever lived. He learned to pitch by hurling rocks at birds when he was growing up. When a shortstop throw caught him between the eyes, he was out cold for two days. When he came around, he had double vision. He kept throwing until his vision came back. I 'm waiting for my vision to come back as I watch Bailey Hutchinson get into his jacked-up black F150 with the Confederate flag on the bumper and the yellow *Don't Tread on Me Sticker*.

He jumps up like a cowboy and fires up his truck and roars around the parking lot, and then like Fernando, leaves me with nothing but a bad feeling. I put my bat bag in Mom's old minivan, which is now mine. when I see someone walking toward me with a cigar and a big hand. He has red hair and this freckled face that is even redder than his hair. I know who he is just by the way he walks. He has MLB all over him.

"Jigger Hix," he says.

We shake hands.

"I scout for the Cubs," he continues. "I been watching you all year."

He says it just like that.

"Kane County Cougars is their farm team, but you might just skip that from what I've seen. Yes, sir. You might."

I just can't believe he's talking to me after what had happened with Bailey. Jigger follows my line of vision as that big black Ford pickup rolls around like it's circling us.

"Yeah, he's fast," he says, reading my mind. Then Jigger turns to me with this red face and gums his cigar. "But like I said, I been watching you since last year...I like your pitching. I really do, and I think the Cubs might like it too, if you finish the year strong....What, you're a senior?"

I stare at him like I had fallen asleep.

"Yeah...a senior...yes, sir."

He pauses, squinting his two blue marbles.

"Was that Jack Langford I saw you talking to?'

"Yes ,sir." I nod. "He's my stepdad."

Jigger Hix guffaws and stamps his foot and shakes his head. He stares where the Pitcher and Mom had driven off, as if he expects them to come back.

"I'll be damned. Now isn't that something." He shakes his head and sucks on his cigar, and it's then I realized he's the same age as the Pitcher. Or at least close.

"He was one of the greats. Yes, sir, he was...and you say he is your stepdad?"

"Yes, sir."

"Is that right?" His blue eyes twinkle. "I should have known that....your stepdad. I guess I know now where you get your pitching style."

"Yes, sir. "

Jigger Hix crosses his arms and taps his cigar toward me.

"I'll bet you have colleges crawling all over you now, don't you"

I shrug and nod.

"Yes, sir...some."

Jigger keeps his arms crosses and nods slowly.

"Hmm...well, now that is honorable. Yes, sir, it is. I never want to get between a man and his college education."

I shrug, and I am a wound-up clock just ringing and ringing, and I don't want anyone or anything to shut off what is happening.

"I'm not sure if I'm going to college or not," I say.

Jigger spits in the dust again.

"Is that right? Well I'll tell you, Ricky, these are big decisions." He spits in the dust again the way the Pitcher does. And it's then I see the bulge in his cheek. He gums the cigar again.

"Many a player has gone straight to the majors. Sometimes the postman only rings once, you know. For me he only rang once, and I am glad I went when he did."

"Yes, sir," I say, not quite sure what he is saying.

"And you want to be there when he rings. You know what I mean? You don't want to miss your moment."

I nod and meet his eyes that feel like they're crawling all over me.

"My dream has always been to pitch for the Cubs in Wrigley Field," I blurt out.

Jiggers' eyebrows go high.

"Well, is it now? Maybe I can help you with that, too. I think that is a very good dream, and I think with a talent like yours, the sky is the limit. The one thing you don't want do is anything that will hurt that arm,' he says patting my shoulder.

"No, sir."

"And you don't want to miss the train when it pulls out. College is a good thing for most people—but maybe not for everyone. When someone has a talent like you have, then they have to look at things differently. You know what I mean?"

"Yes, sir."

"Alright then. We will be in touch, and I'll be watching you finish up."

He puts his hand out, and we shake. His hand feels like iron. Jigger cocks his head and says a funny thing that puts ice into my veins.

"That Bailey Hutchinson was something. We don't want too many of those now, do we?'

"No, sir," I mutter.

Jigger winks and hits me lightly in the shoulder.

"You'll get him next time."

"Take care of that arm," he says back, walking over to a dusty White Cadillac.

And I stare at that Cadillac and wonder if this is the way Mickey Mantle felt when a man pulled up to a field in Oklahoma and told him to get in, like a whole other world had just driven in and if I didn't get in that car, I would be left behind. The postman really might only ring once.

8

DID YOU KNOW THE Star-Spangled Banner wasn't played before games before the Chicago Cubs played the Boston Red Sox in Comiskey Park during World War I? Everyone started singing spontaneously when they played it, and from then on it was played at every game. Boston won, of course. I can hear The Star-Spangled Banner now in the garage. The Pitcher is in there, and it is just like before. The television in the corner is playing, and the fan is rolling, and Shortstop is sleeping in the corner. And the Good Times are by the Lazy Boy he brought over when he moved in.

The only new thing is the plasma screen mounted on the wall. It lights up the whole garage, and the Pitcher is drinking and smoking and keeping an eye on the door because he promised Mom he would cut down on smoking and drinking and Skoal.

"Hey," he says as I duck under the garage.

And it's like I'm not seventeen anymore, but like four years ago looking for the answers again. The mystery that is a Major League Baseball player is back, and I wonder again how he did it.

"Hey," I say back.

"Get yourself a Coke," he says motioning to the old refrigerator he rolled over on a dolly. "Maybe it will get you out of your funk.'"

I stand up and get the Coke.

"Who says I'm in a funk," I mutter.

The Pitcher spits into a can of beer and stares at me with his right eye.

"I saw your playing. You better be in a funk, or we are both in trouble."

I take the ice cold Coke and slump down in the other La-Z-Boy that is well worn and very comfortable. The fan is blowing, and the crickets are outside the garage door, and Shortstop is groaning in his sleep. We sit there and watch the Sox and the Brewers play for a few minutes. The Pitcher lights a cigarette and looks over.

"That scout talk to you?"

I frown and look at him.

"How did you know?"

The Pitcher stretches out his long legs and coughs.

"I been there....remember? Those guys broadcast from a million miles away who they are. I figured he probably wanted to talk to you. They all want to talk to the next hot pitcher."

"They should talk to that Bailey kid," I grumble.

"We feeling sorry for ourselves?"

"Maybe," I say, shrugging.

I look down at my Coke and see my dream down there in that dark fizzy syrup. It is just popping away, and soon it will be gone if I don't get going. The Pitcher lifts his eyebrows and gestures to the television.

"I'd talk to that Bailey kid if I was a scout. He's fast ,and he can hit."

"Great. Maybe I should give him his number," I mutter.

"Maybe you should."

This is not making me feel better. The high of Jigger Hix has been replaced with the hell that is Fernando, and the fact a ninety-plus pitcher has just smoked me. Usually sitting in the garage lifts my spirits, but now I feel antsy and unsure.

"He just moved in from Texas," I murmur.

The Pitcher raises his eyebrows and spits Skoal in a Good Times can. Mom asked him why he drank that cheap beer when there were so many others out there. He said he didn't see why he should pay more for beer that was the same swill as any other. The Pitcher shifts his legs.

"I faced a lot of rock-heads from Texas, and half of them couldn't hit the fly off a fence post, but some of them were the guys I faced later,"

"Thanks a lot."

The Pitcher shrugs.

"Just saying."

Shortstop groans and rolls over. I can hear a car go by and someone walking a dog outside the garage. I think about Joey, who I never really see anymore. He started hanging with some guys who I do not hang with. You know. And ever since college scouts started talking to me, he gets a funny look on his face. Like there was something nobody told him about. He's pretty much the gangbanger, and he does his thing and I do mine, but still it bothers me that we aren't really good friends anymore.

"The MLB guy was from the Cubs," I say.

The Pitcher turns and nods slowly.

"There you go. That's your dream, right?"

I shrug.

"Yeah."

I pause and stare at the pictures of The Pitcher. Like I said, Mom put the good ones in the house, but the others she put up in this perfect row. I stare at the one where he is standing with a bat over his shoulders, looking like a young Joe DiMaggio. I turn back in and look at the Pitcher.

"He asked if I was going to college."

The Pitcher ashes his cigarette.

"What'd you tell him?'

"I said I don't know."

He goes back to the game and doesn't say anything. I watch the smoke float into the television light and breathe heavily. I look at him.

"You ever want to go to college?'

The Pitcher shifts in his chair and picks up his beer.

"Never thought about it."

I frown.

"How come?'

"'Cause guys like me either played ball or went to work

digging ditches," the Pitcher answers. "Times were different then. Most people went to work."

I nod slowly.

"Good thing you played ball, huh."

"Good thing."

I sip my Coke and watch the game for a moment.

"So...Fernando's back."

"Yeah. He's going to blow his johnson off with that gun if he's not careful."

I laugh pretty hard at that.

"Yeah," I say wiping my eyes.

The Pitcher turns then and cocks one eyebrow.

"They always come out of the woodwork if they smell money. You are going to get a lot more of that before it is over. Everyone became my best friend when I went to the MLB, and before that, they didn't want to know me."

"Yeah."

I cross my arms and stare at my bat bag.

"The scout guy says I gotta finish strong."

"Of course." The Pitcher tips his ash in a can of Good Times. "Otherwise, they don't want you. They gotta know you can be consistent."

I finger the Coke and look at the Pitcher holding a cigarette by his cheek.

"He says the postman might only ring once."

"They usually do."

"What do you think?'

The Pitcher stubs his cigarette and mutes the television. Then he looks over.

"I think you been drinking your own Kool-Aid. You gotta quit listening to people telling you you're great. When a kid like that Bailey comes along, you realize you ain't so great, and you got work to do. So now you know. You want your dream, then you gotta keep getting better. You can't rest, Ricky. Ever. That ain't the way it works. Not until you're sitting where I am. Then you can rest all you want, and by the way, then you don't want to. So you figure it out.'

The Pitcher turns the television back on, and I feel better. Yeah. I know what he said is the truth. You do gotta keep working all the time, but sometimes you gotta hear it. I finish my Coke and stand.

"Thanks."

He coughs again, hacks is more like it. He spits into his beer can.

"Just don't tell your mother I was smoking and drinking again."

I frown and stare at The Pitcher.

"Are you kidding? Mom knows everything."

9

EVEN BEFORE THE CHICAGO White Sox threw the 1919 Series, they were called the Black Sox. That was because Charles Comiskey, the owner, charged them to wash their uniforms. So they quit washing them, and they got dirtier and dirtier until the sports writers called them the Black Sox. Comiskey was one of the reasons the White Sox threw the game. He took all the money, and everyone knew something was going to happen. Like I knew something was going to happen when I walked in the door.

When I come in, Mom is watching The Voice. She digs the way people sing, and then the dudes in the chairs pick the best one. I can't stand all the screaming, and the people all sound the same to me. But she snaps it off when I walk in, and she tells me to put away my bat bag and kick off my shoes at the door and take a shower and all the usual mom stuff. She is laying back on the couch with a glass of wine. It's funny. The Pitcher does his thing in the garage with ball games, and Mom does hers with The Voice or Glee or Breaking Bad. Guess everyone has their thing.

"Fernando's back, huh?'

Mom is smoking and keeping an eye on the door so the

Pitcher won't catch her. Mom's eyes flash over. Yeah, we both knew why Fernando had come back. Sort of like a storm that appears when conditions are just right. Well, conditions were pretty good. Son is going to be an MLB pitcher. Yeah, time for lightning to strike.

"Let me worry about him," Mom says stubbing her cigarette in a ceramic ashtray she keeps hidden.

"Sure."

But I know this is just talk. Nobody can handle Fernando.

"Have you studied for your ACTs," Mom wants to know.

"I'm going to study tonight."

"Have you done your biology?'

"Tonight."

"Uh-huh."

Here's the deal, and don't tell anyone, but I might not graduate. I wasn't lying before when I said I make mostly *Cs*. But when you add in a couple *Ds* and *Fs*, well, I mean it's going to be close. My grades never really kicked it in, and Mr. Fenstorm, my biology teacher, has it in for me. I mean, I don't pass Biology, then it is game over. No graduation. Hey, Bobby Jenks flunked out of high school, and he pitched one hundred-three. Guess he drank a lot after that, but he made it, you know. They say he hit hard times after the Sox won the Series. Still, I could take those hard times, you know, after pitching in a World Series with Ozzie Guillen calling me out to close him down.

Mom lifts her head and stares at me. I can feel the mom vibes.

"What?"

"Esmeralda called." Mom frowns. "She said you haven't returned her calls."

I shrug.

"We broke up. She dumped a Coke on my head."

Mom sits up and examines me.

"Why was that?'

I stand with my bat bag and shrug again.

"I don't know. I guess she was pretty mad about something, "I mutter.

Mom's eyes are like lasering into my head. I swear she can read my mind.

"And what did you do to get a Coke dumped on your head?"

"Diet Coke."

"Alright. A Diet Coke then."

I shrug about a thousand times and look everywhere but at her and kick the carpeting with my toe and talk down to the floor. I grumble with words that she cannot understand.

"Talk clearly, Ricky."

"I just did."

"No, you didn't."

Shrugging and muttering, I finally say, "I guess I told her I wasn't taking her to prom."

Mom's eyes are on fire now. Her whole body is moving, and she is soaring around the room, throwing lightning bolts that I am starting to dodge.

"Ricky!" she screams. "She already bought the dress!"

This I know, and this I know will be Mom's weapon of choice. Major guilt, but I have armored myself up, and I am already sidestepping the bolts. I roll my shoulders three times and let roll another bomb.

"Yeah, I know, but I had asked Christine and I couldn't take both of them."

Mom is now off the couch. Not good. She is staring at me like I am a murderer or something. Scratch that. *Mass murderer.*

"Christine? And who did you ask first, Ricky?"

"What difference does that make?"

"It makes all the difference in the world, Ricky!

The shrug again, then the mumble, then the stare out the window, then the step toward the door.

"Ricky! Who did you ask first?'

Man, Mom is a pit bull. Once she grabs on, she does not let go. I breathe heavily. It's like I'm in court and things are not going my way, you know. I know I am going to jail.

"Es...but then I asked Christine," I point out weakly.

Mom shakes her head and wonders what she did wrong, then she crosses her arms and stares at me like I'm the devil.

"You should have never had done that to Esmeralda, Ricky."

I shut my eyes and feel a pain in the front of my eyes. This is not what I need right now. Not while I have Bailey Hutchinson breathing down my neck.

"Mom! Christine is like a cheerleader! She is like the most popular girl in high school, and she's rich and hot, and Mexican dudes like me don't usually get a chance to date someone like her!"

None of that floats in Mom land. It's like my boat is taking on so much water, I can't even bail anymore. Mom is nodding "Uh-huh," she says. "Well, Mexican dudes like you should not be asking other girls when you have already committed to someone else."

I wave my hand.

"Mom. Es can go with someone else."

"Oh, you broke her heart, you bad boy," Mom declares.

Bad boy? Now we are going way back in time.

I really want to get out of here because I have run out of bullets and Mom is clearly winning.

"You treated her badly, Ricky."

Guilt. Guilt. Guilt. It is coming down in buckets.

"Ahhhhh," I say. "You don't know what it's like when a chick like Christine says she wants to go out with you, Mom. You just don't get it!"

Mom's eyes have gone berserk, and her curly brown hair is up in arms.

"And why do you think she wants to go out with you?"

I stare at Mom and break into a smile.

"Because I am *the man*."

Mom's eyes dull, and she shakes her head.

"Really, Ricky? *The man*? You're the man?"

"Yes. I am," I say not at all sure that I am the man.

Mom shakes her head, wagging her finger.

"You are the not *the man,* and this Christine will dump you, and you will be less than *the man*."

I shake my head.

"You just don't get it Mom."

"Uh-huh." She goes back to the couch. "I do get it, and you better take a hard look at your actions. That Esmeralda is three times the girl Christine is."

"You don't even know Christine, Mom."

Mom nods.

"I know enough. I know that when something better comes

along, she won't remember your name."

I hoist up my bat bag and shake my head.

"Nothing better is coming along, Mom."

"Tell that to Bailey Hutchinson," she says coolly.

Wow. Knockout punch. Slam. I stop and turn slowly.

"Low blow, Mom."

"Really? You should know all about that," she says.

10

JOE DIMAGGIO MARRIED MARILYN Monroe, and everyone thought he was the luckiest guy in the world. Even after they had been divorced for years, he said she was the only woman who ever broke his heart. I get that. I mean, Marilyn was the most beautiful woman in the world. And to me, Christine is the most beautiful girl in the world. Mom never says anything, but whenever I bring her up, she gets a funny look in her eyes. And I know what she is thinking, because I had dinner at Christine's with her father and mother in their big house in the rich section of Jacksonville. Their house was like a mansion with all these old things and paintings. Even their dog was expensive.

We sat at this big long table, and her parents stared at me.

"Christine tells me you are quite a pitcher," her dad says in his red tie and white shirt.

I guess he is some kind of big lawyer dude who knows a lot of people, because there are all these pictures of him shaking hands with famous people.

"Yes, sir," I say eating, but I wasn't hungry at all.

"She says there are professional scouts looking at you."

"Yes, sir," I say nodding, watching the Mexicans working outside on their lawn.

Christine's mother looks like some kind of lady from television. All this blond hair piled up, and red lips. She looks down the table at me. The whole house looks like something from that old show *Rich and Famous*.

"Is it a Mexican team?"

Where do you go with that? But I just play along and laugh.

"Mother!" Christine says.

Her mother turns and says in this voice that is like china or something.

"Well, I don't know, dear."

"No, ma'am. It's the Cubs," I say

Her dad leans back and puts these big hands on the table with gold cufflinks.

"Maybe you will do for pitching what Roberto Clemente did for right field." He was just throwing out a Mexican ball player.

"Yes, sir. I'll take that," I say smiling like the happy Mexican still watching the guys outside on their riding mowers with weed-whackers strapped to their backs. And I wonder what the difference is between them and me right then. I mean, why am I not out there, and why are they? Is it because I'm still in high school or because I pitch so well?

Christine's parents stare at my old minivan a long time and keep looking in the living room where we sit after dinner. Her father asks me to take a walk with him. We walk down his driveway, and he really looks like those dudes on the news with perfect hair and blue eyes.

"My daughter is going to college," he says like he's talking about the weather.

"Yes, sir."

He pauses then and turns with his eyes like two bullets. I mean, it was like a dark cloud appeared, and the Mexican glare rolled in with the rain. .

"And I know to her you're exotic."

Exotic? Like an animal? So now my heart is thumping like crazy, just bamming away, and I want to get back in my van and drive away because this is not good.

"I don't know what you mean," I say.

He smiles, staring at his cigar.

"I mean you are not the type of boy we usually see Christine dating. You are the first Mexican-American she has dated for one thing."

"That is a good thing, right, sir?"

He keeps this strange smile on his face.

"Well, things usually go better when people of the same background stay together. I am sure you have girls that are similar in background, and you are very comfortable with them."

Now my face is like red ,man. I mean bright red, and my heart is pounding.

"I am comfortable with Christine."

He laughs lightly. "I am sure you are. But I am not concerned with whether or not you are comfortable with her Ricky. I am concerned with her future. When you have children, you will understand this."

I swallow and frown and speak through my teeth that are clenched.

"I don't think I understand what you are saying, sir."

He loses the smile and looks at me again like I have a gun.

"Then let me put it to you plainly. Like should stay with like."

"You mean because I am Mexican?"

He then puffs his cigar with his eyes smoking as well.

"I hope things work out for you, Ricky. You people have a hard time of it, I know, and baseball might be your opportunity to get out of your...circumstances." And then he pulls the cigar out of his mouth and stares at me. "But if you don't behave yourself with my daughter, I will hunt you down. You will not escape me, so don't even think about it."

I cannot speak. I cannot move. It's like if I do, I will start screaming.

"Do we understand each other, Ricky Hernandez?"

I look at him then and nod.

"Yeah...I get you," I say.

"Good."

He puts the cigar back in his mouth and walks back up the driveway.

Christine asked me about a hundred times what he said, but I just said he wanted to talk about baseball. So I get why Mom is suspicious. She can smell somebody who has it in for Mexicans and probably figures Christine is not my type. And maybe she isn't, but I got to find that out myself, because when I'm with her, I feel like a million bucks.

11

SHOELESS JOE JACKSON COULD neither read nor write, but he could hit. He came from a mill and became one of the biggest hitters of all time. He hit with a bat called *Black Betsy* made from a Northern Hickory tree coated with coat after coat of Jackson's tobacco juice. He learned to bat from an old Confederate who learned baseball in a Union prison camp. He was called Shoeless Joe Jackson after he was spotted playing in the Minors barefoot because his new shoes were too tight. He was banished forever after the White Sox Scandal.

The way I am feeling banished when I see Esmeralda sitting with Mom three days later. She is sitting at the kitchen table and I can hear Mom and her talking, and I consider just walking out the front door. Mom and Es have always hung together. Her parents are pretty lame, so she was always over at our house telling Mom her problems. And I know her play now. It's only been a week since I broke up with her, and the whole prom thing and all, and I know she is telling Mom what an asshole I am. So I turn around and figure I will hang in the garage.

"Ricky?"

"Yeah," I say with this sinking feeling.

"Esmeralda is here, Ricky."

Big deal is what I want to say, but I just mutter.

"Oh, great."

"Come in and say hello, Ricky."

I groan. I am so toast now, man. Esmeralda knows how to play people, and she is playing my mom against me all the way. So I go into the hall and then into the kitchen.

"Hey, Es," I mutter.

She smiles.

"Hi, Ricky," she says, like she just happened to stop by or something.

Her hair is still pinned up McDonald's style and her gum is rolling between her teeth. She even looks like Mom with this curly black hair and the same fiery dark eyes. She can go ghetto faster than even Mom when she gets mad. They are drinking coffee, and both look at me like I am some kind of zoo animal.

"Who gave you a ride, Ricky?" Mom asks setting down her cup.

"Joey," I answer.

"Joey, huh," Es says, her eyes flashing. "I hear he is a gangbanger now. "

"Nah...he just plays it up," I say, shaking my head.

Mom is on fire now.

"Don't you go near him if he is in a gang, Ricky!"

Esmeralda is watching me, and her eyes have gone smug.

"You don't take any more rides with him, do you hear me?"

I stare at Es, who is trying to look all innocent.

"I just heard he was in a gang now. Maybe I'm wrong," she says, shrugging.

"You are wrong," I say giving her the glare.

"You stay away from him, Ricky. He is headed for prison or heaven."

"He's my best friend, Mom," I point out.

Mom's head is going side to side.

"Not any more. You want to end up shot?"

I breathe tiredly. Old girlfriend trap. That is what I just walked into. And she is using my mom to spring it, which really pisses me off.

"I'm not going to end up shot, Mom," I mumble.

"You will if you let him drive you around. Ever since he dropped out of high school, I knew he would end up in the gangs."

Mom then narrows in on me.

"And you better be working on your biology!"

"I'm working on it," I mutter.

"Uh-huh."

Esmeralda looks like one of those people at a ball game just enjoying the show. This is total payback for dumping her and not taking her to prom.

"If you don't pass biology, then you won't go to college," Mom declares. The truth is Mom is right, and a bigger truth is I would not even be in school if it wasn't for her. She didn't homeschool me, but she might as well have because she is the one who taught me, not the teachers.

"Maybe I'm not going to college then."

Mom is now sitting back, and her chin is starting to bob.

"Oh, you are going to the Major Leagues? I haven't heard anyone waving a contract in your face. "

"Yeah, Ricky, you want to go to college," Esmeralda say with a chin bob that matches her.

"He has this crazy notion of going to play for a team and not going to these schools offering him all this money."

Esmeralda turns and looks at me with her bright red lipstick and her ponytail swishing.

"You mean they are giving you money, and you won't go? What kind of thing is that?" She says with her head bobbing and weaving. Mom follows, gesturing to me like I am not even there.

"I told him that. He is crazy! I told him you need an education."

"Of course, he does."

They are both bobbing and weaving, and it is like I am have left the room or something.

"These boys are all nuts, you know. "

"Oh, I know, Mrs. H. I know. Look at what we girls have to put with."

"I wouldn't do it. I would find yourself a nice white boy and leave these crazy Mexican boys alone."

Chin bob. Weave. Chin bob. Crazy eyes. They are like trying to outdo each other in ghetto anger.

"I have thought about it. Some of them even ask you to prom and then back out at the last minute, Mrs. H."

Mom shakes her head.

"That is horrible. What kind of boy would do that?"

Esmeralda turns and stares at me.

"A bad one, Mrs. H. A bad one."

So now they have forgotten about me, and I am like tiptoeing down the hall to the garage. I open the door and slip into the garage. Now I know how Shoeless Joe felt when he ended up running a liquor store in South Carolina. Some kind of mix between shame and remorse.

12

HONUS WAGNER PLAYED FOR the Boston Pirates and was probably the best player there ever was. He could hit and field like no tomorrow, and nobody could stop him. He had long arms and a barrel chest, and they said he threw so hard that when he threw a ball to first base, the pebbles he scooped with the ball got there first. That's what Bailey was like to me, and those pebbles were hitting me everywhere.

The Pitcher is having a smoke and coughing up a lung. Lately, I have noticed he has a hell of a smoker's hack. Mom is all over him to quit and he does, but then he goes right back to it. Just like his beers. He falls on and off the wagon all the time. But it's not like he gets drunk anymore, he just has enough, he says, to take the edge off.

"So you walked into the trap?" he asks without looking up.

He is wearing the same old canvas shorts and a golf shirt. Mom says he would wear the same clothes every day if she didn't put out his clothes on the bed. I get that. I would do that, too. Pitchers don't care what they wear, the same way they don't really care about money or what other people think of them. You just care about the ball, man.

"Yeah," I say flopping down in the other chair.

The Pitcher ashes his cigarette and gestures to the television.

"Your team is getting stomped by the Yankees."

I shrug.

"So what's new?"

The Pitcher frowns and shakes his head.

"Yeah, the Cubs don't win...but they always fill Wrigley Field."

"That's because it's one of the last great parks," I point out.

"That and Fenway," he says.

I get up and get a Coke out of the refrigerator. We watch the ballgame for a few minutes.

"So your mother says you aren't taking Esmeralda to the prom," he says not taking his eyes off the game.

I turn with the Coke in my mouth. This surprises the hell out of me. The Pitcher never really talks about stuff like girls or anything except pitching or the car or keeping my room clean.

"Uh-huh," I murmur.

He tilts his head and cocks his right eyebrow.

"She's a nice girl."

"Uh-huh."

I don't say anything, and see the bucket of rocks in the corner of the garage. Sometimes, I'll go out to the garage and just pick up the rocks just to see how they feel. It's almost like they are holy or something. I wish I was throwing them now. Ever since Bailey, I feel like I am floating on very thin air.

"I hear you are taking someone else," the Pitcher continues.

"Uh-huh."

The Pitcher nods slowly and puckers his lips..

"I ain't much in this department, but all I got to say is, don't drink your own Kool-Aid."

I frown.

"What do you mean?'"

"You know what I mean."

I shake my head.

"No, I don't."

The Pitcher swigs his Good Times.

"Think about it."

"Ricky!"

It's Mom.

"Yeah!" I shout.

"Will you walk Esmeralda home?"

I groan and get out of the chair.

"Why do I gotta do this?" I mutter.

The Pitcher has this thin smile and leans back.

"Everyone gets what they deserve in the end," he says.

13

CHECK THIS OUT. THEY used to leave their baseball gloves in the outfield in the twenties. The opposing team would not trip over them either. They just left them there. Imagine that. Of course, this was about the time they banished the eight White Sox players for life after they put the fix in on the game. Joe Jackson ended up in Greenville, South Carolina, running a liquor store, and nobody even knew who he was after a few years.

Like I don't want Es to know who I am anymore. But she is waiting to pounce. It's been like a week since I told her I wasn't taking her to prom, and she is still pissed. I can tell with her fast walk and her gum moving fast and her eyes that keep rolling my way and then off like she has nothing better to do than walk down the street with me. Her house is only like a couple blocks away, so the whole walk her home thing is just so she can go to town on me.

But I know her play, and I figure on not saying anything t until I reach her porch, and then it will be *Good night, Es,* and then I will turn and walk back home. But she looks at me and knows my game and lets me have it anyway.

"So you dumped me for that stuck-up rich bitch," she says out of the blue.

I do a couple shrugs.

"Yeah."

Es shakes her head.

"She is the kind of bitch we hated all our lives, and now that you the big pitcher, you are going to take her over me?"

I'm rolling my head because, I don't have any response except that in school, news travels fast and once it got around that MLB scouts were calling me, than, yeah, man, I became the dude and suddenly this blond-haired, blue-eyed cheerleader is like talking to me and asking me if I will give her a ride home, and if was I going to prom, and then, I dunno, we were like dating and I just asked her to go to prom and conveniently forget I had asked Es. And the truth is, man, I like Es and always have, and we like grew up together, and I know what I did was shitty, but still, man, you all of a sudden are like given some candy and, what, you don't eat it?

But none of this is helping me right now, because Es is on a roll.

"You just turning into an asshole, Ricky Hernandez. I never thought you would do something like this, but I see now you just going to leave all the people who helped you and go off with some fake stuck-up rich bitch. I don't who you are anymore. I thought you and I had something, and now you break off with me a week before prom, and my dad said he was going to kick your ass, but I told him not to bother because you ain't worth it."

I'm nodding because that is all you can do once Es gets rolling, man. And you know she is right. There is no excuse except that I never have had people telling me I'm *the man* before. Not like this. And yeah, I'm trying out the new car, right? That's what you do when you get a new car. You take it for a spin, man, and that is what I am doing, but right now I feel like I'm driving Mom's minivan because now Es is crying.

"I already had my... dress...you asshole!"

We are stopped now in front of her house, and I am feeling like I want to melt down into the sidewalk, because she is wiping her eyes with the back of her hands and staring off down the street. But I can see these big tears on her cheeks, and I wish I had never met Christine, and in that moment I wish the MLB dudes had never called me. The Pitcher had said once that fame has a price, and maybe I was finding that out already, but I didn't really want to ever hurt Es.

"Look...I'm sorry, Es," I begin.

"You're sorry. That's the best you can do," she sobs.

Her eyes are hot and wet now, and her chin is bobbing. Damn. She does look like my mother sometimes.

"You dump me for this cheerleader white bitch, and all your can say is you are sorry!"

She then hits me in the shoulder, and you know it kind of hurts. Es can pack a punch. Then she hits me again, and I have to step back because she slugs me three more times and then bursts into tears all over again.

"*Asshole. Asshole Asshole!*" she screams.

Then I hear the door open, and there is her dad, Ricardo. He is a big dude with tats and a bushy goatee, and he stares at me like he wants to kill me.

"Esmeralda, come in the house and leave that trash outside," he says.

So she does, and he gives me one more dagger stare and then closes the door. And the trash, it just turns and blows on back home.

14

THE FIRST TWENTY YEARS of baseball belonged to the pitchers. Nobody could hit because the first thing a pitcher would do to the ball was dirty it up or spit on it or get grease on it, and this made it erratic and unhittable. Also, the ball wasn't wound tight so it would cave in when it hit the bat. Hardly anyone got a home run. Then Ray Chapman was beaned in the head by a spitball and died. After that, umpires could call out a ball the second it got dirty and replace it with another. They also wound the balls a lot tighter. Then came Babe Ruth, and baseball belonged to the hitters after that.

And you know one thing always blows into another, like Ray Chapman getting killed and Babe Ruth coming on the scene. Walking home, I hear like this car with a crappy muffler and then this low riding rusted out car is right next to me, and I see Fernando leaning out the window and yelling something. One thing leading to another.

"What?" I shout.

"Get in, man," he shouts back. "I'll give you a ride, man."

Fernando is the last dude I want to see right now, and my heart is like pounding a million miles a minute. Fight or flight or something, man, but when I hear his voice, I feel like running.

Mom says you get that way with people who treat you bad. She says it's like Pavlov's dog, which is something where, I guess, they give dogs some meat even when they shock them. So then they just give the dog the meat, and they won't take it because they know the shock is coming. Fernando is all about the shock.

But now he has pulled over, and his car is a piece of crap. I didn't know they even let cars like that on the road, you know. It's got like one tail light and one headlight, and the tail pipe sparks because it is scraping the road, and it's so loud you can't even hear over it. And now he's out like walking over in his low riders, and he still has on his sunglasses, but its night and like he has grey in his hair and his goatee, and his fat arms are kind of mushy now, and his gut hangs out and he has even more tats all over his chest and neck.

"Hey man...what's happening, bro?" he says, giving me the gang hug.

"Not much," I murmur. I really do want to run. He smells like dope and booze and sweat. He looks like he is living out of his car. I stand there on the sidewalk and wait because Fernando, he doesn't just show up for nothing, man, and I don't have to wait long.

"So you just taking a walk, man?"

"Yeah."

I ain't going to say anything about Esmeralda. The less given, the better with Fernando, you know.

"That's cool." He leans against his car and crosses his arms. "So how's the arm, man?"

I shrug, "It's good."

He does the slow nod.

"Yeah, man. You got it going on." He shakes his head. "I guess if I had worked harder, man, I might of ended up like you, you know."

"Yeah."

Fernando rubs his own arm and spits in the street.

"But you know, I didn't have a World Series pitcher to coach me either, man, like you."

I can feel his stare, and I am thinking about how long it will take me to run down the street into our house.

"I mean, you know,I set you and your mom up, you know, and then she just kicks me aside and marries this dude...I dunno, man...I thought about that a lot in the joint, and it used to really burn me, you know." Fernando looks at me with his dark glasses like black holes in space, you know—no gravity, no mass. "And I figure, man, you know, just let it go and get your due, man, and then everything is cool."

I nod, but I don't feel good.

"So I figure, man, you go MLB. What, they give you a hundred grand or something just to sign, right?"

I shrug. "Nobody has talked about any money."

Fernando stands off the car and points his finger.

"Yeah, but they will, bro. Trust me. Look, man." He spread his arms. "I ain't greedy. I figure you flip me like fifty K,and I figure we are square for everything I did for you, you know. Like fifty grand will be nothing for you, man. "

And it is here, the sting comes. Like a wasp or a bee on the brain and I am like nine and Fernando just hit me for the hundredth time or stolen our money again and maybe that's why I look him in his sorry eye and say, "You never did shit for me."

And we are back, you know, like old times. He loses his fake smile and walks up close.

"Look, you little shit,I could off you, man. So don't f— with me. I was going to try and be cool, but I can see you're going to be the little dick like you always were."

His breath is like in my face, and we are almost nose to nose, and I know his play. He wants me to take a swing so he can try and kick my ass or shoot me or some shit. I can see his nostrils flaring, and he's breathing like a bull, and I wonder then if I can kick his ass. He looks awful flabby, but I also know Fernando doesn't fight fair and probably is packing. Then he steps back and nods.

"Alright, man, we will play it like this. Did you know Maria has been giving me money for the last few years?"

"Bullshit," I say, thinking this is the last thing Mom would do.

"No, man. I got the checks. And it know it ain't hers. It's that old bastard she married, so she wouldn't get her ass deported."

"You're full of it."

Fernando laughs shortly and shows his crappy teeth.

'Uh-huh. Oh, I get it. You think she loved him? You one dumb dude; Maria is slick. She played his ass, man. She saw a meal ticket and a way to stay in the country, and you were just the bait, man. Shit. She played you, too."

I am not liking any of this. Mom has been giving Fernando money? No way. Fernando rolls on.

"Man, she's been sending me like a couple grand a month for years, you know. And I knew she was illegal, but we didn't have the money for the lawyers and shit, but she's got it now." Fernando then stepped up close. "But how do you think that pitcher dude would feel about her giving me his money all these years? I got emails where she talks about playing him, man, for his money."

I stare at him, and now I feel like taking a punch.

"You're lying. "

Fernando raises his arms and shrugs.

"Hey, it's true, and if that dude knew, he would throw the Mexicans right out the door, man. So here it is, bro. You get me my money, or I'm going to that dude and rat out Maria, man, and show him the little lying whore she is."

I step toward him, and just like that, Fernando pulls out his piece. He holds it low by his side like gunslinger. I can see now it's like an old black .38. He holds it pointed toward my waist, and I cannot move. Like I have ice in my veins. I don't think I am even breathing.

"Yeah, you want a piece of this, man?" He smiles. "C'mon, I bust a cap in you like nothing."

Then like I find my voice and surprise myself.

"Put that down, and I'll kick your ass," I say because we both know this is the case now.

Fernando grins again.

"Yeah. Maybe you can, man, but I send your ass to the morgue."

I start walking then, and I hear his crappy laughter behind me.

"Yeah, man. I be back in touch. Fifty-k, man. You come up with it, and we cool. You don't, and I'll let that dude know about the two wetbacks living in his house, man. And maybe I bust a cap on you anyway. "

I just keep walking, and I hear his junker start and then pass me. I watch it turn the corner with one red taillight like some caboose from hell

15

THE 1906 CUBS MIGHT have been the best ever. They won one hundred sixteen games and then the pennant. This is the era of Tinkers, Evers and Chance. They all hated each other but were great. Tinkers was so grouchy, they called him the human crab, and Evers and Chance fought once over cab fare and didn't speak for two seasons. Yet they were a great first baseman, shortstop, and second baseman. And then there was the pitcher Mordecai "Three Fingers" Brown. He lost his fingers in a farm accident, but it gave him a devastating curve ball. He went against Ed Walsh for the White Sox. Walsh was the master of the spitball and put the Sox up by three games. Then five. Then the Cubs lost.

Those guys must have been devastated the way the pitcher was devastated after Mom and him went to the doctor. Ball players have to deal with loss, you know. One bad thing after another can happen to you, and that's why after Fernando, the second bad thing happened. I mean, there has to be a radar or something in the universe, because right after Fernando, I hear the Pitcher and Mom going at it. I mean, they fight sometimes, and part of it is Mom's temper, which is pretty bad. And some of it is the Pitcher, who is one stubborn dude. But they are really going at it in the garage when I walk up, and I stop on the sidewalk and just stand there.

Mom is doing the pitching like Three Fingers Brown, and the Pitcher is giving it back like Evers.

"You are still smoking after what the doctor told you?"

"What does it matter? If I got it, I got it," he retorts.

"That is bullshit," Mom screams, and you can hear her all the way down the street. I mean, she is loud when she gets going. Then The Pitcher coughs like he's hacking up a lung. I have noticed his cough has not gotten better, but it hasn't slowed him down, and it sure hasn't stopped him from smoking cigarettes. Mom is standing in front of him and holding her arms wide.

"You see....you see what you are doing to yourself?"

"Maria, I've smoked my whole life, and what I do now won't make a difference," he says.

"How do you know that? They haven't even biopsied it yet!"

And I just get cold, you know. I mean, I really hate that word biopsy, man. It like equals death to me, and I know a lot of people have them and they turn out okay, but a lot of people, it means the end, man. And now the Pitcher is coughing again, and I know what they are talking about. The big *C*. Seems like everybody gets it now. Mom says it's because of all the stuff people eat and the environment. And smoking.

"I got it," he growls.

"You don't know that."

The Pitcher looks up at her and says in a clear voice.

"Maria, don't bullshit a bullshitter. If I want to smoke and chew tobacco, then no rock-head doctor is going to tell me different."

"I think I remember someone telling me I was an idiot for not going to the doctor."

"Yeah, that was different."

"Oh, really? How?"

"It just was. They could help you."

"They could help you, too, if you get your head out of your ass."

"No, they can't."

This sends Mom, and she paces back and forth, shaking

her head. She stops and looks at him and then shakes her head again, going back and forth. Then she stops and screams, "You are being an idiot!"

The Pitcher shrugs. "Maybe so."

And then their voices get low, and I am shaking. I mean, like I am freezing and it is that night four years ago when Mom was sick and the Pitcher carried her to his car. I had that same chattering thing with my teeth, and the thing is it is really warm out, but you know, sometimes you just get cold inside and there is nothing you can do about it. So I walk around the block a couple times. It's one of those baseball nights, you know, warm and airy like a big open ball field, and so I let myself go and see myself on the mound in Wrigley and I'm mowing them down again, and it's 1906 and I am coming into save the day. Just like Three Fingers Brown, but even then it wasn't enough. Walsh pitched a shutout with his spitball, and that was that.

Even Tinkers, Ever and Chance couldn't save them.

16

BABE RUTH SMOKE, DRANK and threw rocks at cops as a boy. His dad beat him. Then they sent him off to a reformatory, where he stayed until he was nineteen. They didn't visit him, and the other boys taunted him and called him nigger lips. He was taught to play baseball by a priest named Father Mathias. He wanted to hit the same way Mathias hit. Ruth soon became the best amateur league pitcher in Baltimore. The Baltimore Orioles signed him to a contract as a pitcher. They had no idea he could hit.

Like I had no idea the Pitcher was so sick. So I go into the house because it is quiet now, and I can hear the Pitcher's television. Mom is washing dishes, which is what she always does when she's mad. Sometimes, she'll rewash just about every dish in the house. I go in and sit on the couch. No way I'm gonna say anything about seeing Fernando.

"Are you going to start on your homework? You know graduation is two weeks away."

She says this without turning around.

"Yeah, I'm going to start now."

"Ricky," she turns. "You are flunking three classes. If you don't pass, then you can't graduate."

I nod slowly. I'm like flunking four, but you know, I was always flunking classes and then somehow I just squeak through with Mom's help. But now I don't know. I can't really believe I'm going to graduate, and then I say what I shouldn't have.

"Maybe I'll just play baseball."

Mom is staring at me, and she turns slowly.

"Really. I notice that man is not calling you back. What are you going to do if it doesn't happen?"

I shrug.

"I'll play on a team somewhere."

Mom is turning red, and I know this burns her.

"You will end up working at McDonald's, Ricky."

"No, I won't," I say, shaking my head.

Mom walks across the room and faces me, and I know I am catching the blowback.

"Really? How many Bailey Hutchinsons are there in the world? Did you ever think about that?"

"I don't know what you mean."

Mom gestures to the ceiling.

"I mean you are living in a *fantasy world,* Ricky. There are lots of pitchers out there who are just as good as you!"

I shake my head.

"No, there aren't."

"Uh-huh. Well, he sure struck you out."

I stare at Mom and feel the blood in my face. Then I look down and take a breath. Mom is just trying to get to me so I'll do my homework. I get that. And she is pissed because the Pitcher won't go to the doctor. But how does she know what I can do? I don't even know. Like Babe Ruth didn't know and the Orioles didn't know. So I just throw it back to her.

"What's wrong with the Pitcher?"

Mom pauses and looks down, and I can see she is really scared.

"What do you mean? He is fine."

I stare at her.

"I heard you guys arguing in the garage."

She breathes heavy, and then her eyes get wet.

"They saw something on a chest X-ray. They have to do a biopsy."

I nod slowly.

"When they going to do it?"

Mom shrugs.

"Ask him. He won't set an appointment with the doctor."

I frown.

"Why not?"

Mom breathes heavy again.

"Because he is stubborn."

I look down the hall to the garage.

"That's stupid."

"Tell him."

I pause, then stand up.

"Maybe I will."

He's smoking, of course, when I go into the garage. It's worse than that; he is sitting in a cloud of smoke like he is saying screw you to the world.

"Those are bad for you," I say.

He looks up from his La-Z-Boy and frowns.

"You talked to your mom, I see," he says dryly.

"Maybe."

I sit in the other chair that we rescued from the end of someone's driveway on trash day. The Pitcher hocks into a Skoal can and looks at me with bloodshot eyes. The creases down his forehead and around his eyes look bad. But his hands are still steady, and he keeps a baseball in his left hand like a talisman.

"Who's playing?"

"New York and Boston."

We watch the Yankees for a few minutes get the Red Sox out of the inning.

His pictures still talk to me in the night. They are more faded now. One is cracked. The others are crooked. The crickets outside and old Shortstop sleeping on his side are part of the garage. His ashes his cigarette, then coughs and hacks into a can of Good Times.

"This guy can't pitch," he grumbles.

I watch the Yankee pitcher throw a curve, then a fastball and get the batter out.

"Seems like he did alright to me."

"Nah, he told the guy what he was going to pitch. The batter was just too stupid to see it."

I pause, then look at him.

"Like somebody too stupid not to go see the doctor."

His eyes roll over to me.

"I saw him, and he saw me."

"And?"

He shrugs and ashes his cigarette.

"And that's it. He saw something, and I figure it won't make a difference now anyway. I played the game my way, and I'll finish it my way."

"That's stupid."

"I told you in the beginning the whole world is a full count against you. It is what it is."

"Bull!"

"My game," he says, looking at me.

I rub my forehead. I forgot how stubborn pitchers can be.

"So you won't go see him?"

"No."

"That's really stupid," I say again." What if my mom had taken your attitude?"

"That's different."

 I shake my head.

"Don't be a rock-head. You owe it to Mom."

The Pitcher looks down his nose at me.

"Now you're pitching at my head, and it ain't going to do you any good."

"You'd say the same thing to her. You did say the same thing," I point out.

"That was different," he says quietly.

I stare at him.

"How was that different?"

"She needed help."

"So do you!"

Then it hit me. The Pitcher had probably never asked for help in his life. As a rule, pitchers don't like to ask anything from anybody. Even when they need it. They are used to pitching through pain, death, war, poverty, and they just don't talk about it. The pitcher code is you play close to your vest and never let anyone see what you really want.

"You should get the biopsy."

He shakes his head and stares at the television.

"Ain't going to happen."

And I knew then it wouldn't happen. It doesn't matter if he was dying. This was his play. The Pitcher would never do the cancer thing anyway. You know, waste away from the drugs. He would go out the way he wanted. The same way he always pitched the way he wanted. It was what made him great, and who could argue with that, you know? I mean, you don't win a World Series by doing what is expected.

17

BABE RUTH WAS TRADED to the Red Sox, where he pitched in a World Series. He held the record for scoreless innings at twenty-nine, and that record stood for forty years. He shouted in the club house: "*I told you I could beat those National League bums!*" Then he began to hit. He modeled his swing after the best power hitter in the game, Shoeless Joe Jackson. He could eat more than anyone else and married a sixteen-year-old waitress.

So now I'm living high like Babe Ruth. I'm getting picked up for school by Christine, who is driving her white BMW. I mean, it is a little weird that I don't pick her up, but she has this killer ride, and I have gotten used to her driving. She rolls to a stop in front of my house with some Rhianna playing. *Oh no no...what you want...oh no no what you want what you want...* And her hair is like platinum, man, and the sunroof is open and she is smiling with her Ray Bans, and she is like a picture of what a rich white chick looks like. And she is my girlfriend, which is something I still can't get used to.

I get in and she gives me a big kiss on the lips, and that gets me ticking, man. And then I lay back in those leather seats, and it is one of the nicest rides I have ever been in. Her phone rings and I kick back and watch the world roll by, thinking of what Fernando said and what I heard in the garage. It's like all the bad shit doesn't exist in this car. Like rich people never have anything bad happen, and I guess that is why everyone wants to be rich.

"Oh, yeah, he is cute. He just moved in from Texas is what I heard," she says in the phone.

I look at Christine.

"I know....I know...well, he's pretty good...got that whole cowboy thing going on....hmmm...hmmm...Bailey, I think....did you see that bitching truck?"

Like every light on my dashboard is going off, and I hold up my hand.

'Whoa. Whoa. Whoa," I say.

Christine glances at me like she forgot I was in the car.

"Gotta go."

She puts down her phone and smiles. I stare at her.

"Are you talking about that Bailey dude from last night?"

She shrugs and looks in the mirror.

"Yeah, he's cute."

I am like wagging with my mouth open.

"What the hell. Why don't you just go out with him then?" I say.

Christine frowns

"You aren't jealous, are you?"

I shake my head because I want to get back to playing like I don't care.

"No, but damn. You 're talking about him and all."

"Well, he certainly is a good baseball player," she murmurs.

I stare at her, feeling my face getting warm.

"What is that supposed to mean?"

"Nothing," she says turning into the school parking lot.

She turns the car off and looks at me.

"I wonder if he'll get drafted like you."

I can't even breathe. It's like Bailey is in the car with us, and then like on cue this black pick up wheels in next to us, and this dude with this black hat is staring down at me from the truck. He grins and opens his door and nods.

"Hey, Mex," Bailey says jumping out like the last cowboy.

18

THERE WAS A GUY NAMED Jim Devlin. He was the first pitcher to ever take money to throw a game and got banned from baseball. For years afterward, he would hang around hoping the owners would take pity on him and let him play again. They never did. He died from consumption two years after he became a cop. I think about that with the Pitcher, and I wonder if some part of him died when he left the mound. Because once you know what it is like to pitch with a crowd behind you, it is hard to forget.

But I'm not thinking about that now. I'm thinking about Bailey Hutchinson and wondering what the hell he is doing at my school, and, more than that, what is he doing in my bullpen. And it is a beautiful day in May. The ball is a white dot against the blue, and the infield is the pure green of some picture that shows you how perfect a lawn can be. And everyone has settled in to watch a game between two teams that are about in the middle. We had won some and lost some, and so had they.

And I am trying to put away the shock of three days before when Bailey popped up in the parking lot and then in the ball field with his fiery helmet. That blue sparkly helmet was something from hell with orange flames trailing behind. And when he ran, it looked like those flames were fanned by the speed of his passage. And when he batted, those flames roared up like a bonfire as he knocked one over the back fence. And when he pitched, those flames came right at you. And I saw no way to extinguish those flames.

Coach said his family moved across town when their house was finished. He only played for East three days before because they were living in an apartment. So he could go to either school. So why pick mine? Why not go back to some school in Texas?

That's what I wanted to ask him with his big cowboy shit-eating grin and those blue eyes that were just like Eric's. They had become instant pals. Eric was always looking for anyone to put against me. He played mostly in the outfield and wasn't even very good at that. So I think he saw Bailey as an answer to a prayer.

And now in the middle of the third inning I knew those fire bolts had done their job. Because I was off. Way off. My fastball was outside and my curve wasn't breaking, and my sinker wasn't sinking and forget about my changeup. The fine-tuning over the years had broken down like someone came in and crossed all the wires. And even as I watched the players rotate around the bags, I knew the person who had crossed those wires was sitting by the coach and waiting.

And after a two-run homer, it wasn't long before those fireballs started smoldering. *Time!* The coach called out, and then he was walking out with Bailey, and I thought, well, there it all goes. There goes everything in the world, and a man with a sparkly helmet and a Texas drawl and a jacked up pickup truck was taking my dream with him. I walked back and sat down on the bench and realized it had been a while since this happened. It had been about three years, but like riding a bicycle, you never forget the feeling. And then I started hearing those cannonballs.

Bailey warmed up like a tank, and the catcher mitt smoked. The batter stood there helpless while fireballs rained down one after another. *Strike One. Strike Two. Strike Three. Batter out!* Then another batter approached tepidly and lifted his bat, and Bailey scorched the wood. He burned the catcher mitt until it was smoking. *Strike one. Strike two. Strike Three...BATTER OUT!* And he trotted off in disgrace while Bailey chewed gum and grinned and tipped his hat to Christine in the stands and then lit up the next batter with flaming curves, fastballs, breaking balls, knuckle balls. And before anyone knew it, that smoldering bat was back in the dugout, and the batter joined the rest of the disgraced players, and Bailey sauntered off as the new sheriff in town.

19

BEFORE BABE RUTH, PITCHERS didn't have to bear down until the later innings of the ball game. When Babe Ruth started playing, pitchers had to bear down right away. There was now the danger of someone getting a homerun with the first pitch of the game. Pitching and baseball were changed forever. I think of this because I have to bear down now or lose everything.

And now Fernando is sitting in the parking lot in his ghetto cruiser. I'm walking toward Mom's old minivan, and he gets out real slowly and walks across the pavement. I had hung around talking to Coach Hoskins, who explained Bailey would be in the rotation. I tried to have a game face and all that, but I felt like getting down on the ground and crying. And this Bailey guy is all Texas polite. *Yes, sir. No, sir. That sounds mighty fine, sir. The team comes first, sir. Whatever is best for the team, sir.* Then he shakes my hand like he's the ambassador of Texas or something.

"I don't want any rivalry between you two. We are a team," Coach Hoskins says.

"Oh, yes, sir. No problem, sir. Only want what is best for the team."

I don't say anything because once Coach Hoskins left, Bailey turns to me with that thin little Texas grin and mutters, "Tough luck, Mex."

And I throw down right there and face him.

"You call me that once more, and I'm going to kick your ass, cowboy!"

He just grins because one of the other coaches has just walked into the locker room. He nods to Bailey and me and heads for the lockers.

"Well see you tomorrow," he broadcasts then drops his voice far down. "Don't look like you going anywhere but down from here...Mex."

And then he just saunters off, and I wait until I think he has taken his black jacked up, chrome wheeled stacked F-150 and left, and that's why it is really just Fernando and I. He walks up while I put my bat bag into the van.

"Hey, man, how come you don't return my texts?"

I shrug.

"Didn't get them," I mutter.

"Bullshit, man. What, you too good now to return my text? You the big man now."

I can smell the weed and booze. Fernando breathes it out like a dragon man. His nostrils are flaring, and I know his eyes are blood red behind his shades. I close the door to the van.

"I just didn't get them," I say again, walking toward the driver's side door. Fernando steps right in my path, and his breath man is hot and bothered.

"Hey, I need some payola, man. I'm sleeping in my car while you and Maria are sponging off that old man."

I shrug and really just want to get into the car because I am tired and I know where this is going.

"I'm busted, man. I don't have any money," I tell him.

"Yeah you know that is bullshit."

I hold my arms wide, thinking how long it will take me to get into the car.

"I am!"

Fernando then reaches into my jean pocket and tries to dig out my wallet. I knock his hand away, and I don't see the right that comes up from his waist. It meets my eye socket and I see stars. Fernando is breathing like a bull, and I can see now he is really juiced. I go down, and he is over me.

"Give me some money, you little shit!"

And it's like old times, right. He is beating up on his kid and looking for money. And my eye is killing me, and I know it will be black and blue, and I realize then I'm bigger than he is. He's standing with his arms wide, and I still got my hand to my eye and I stand up slowly. He doesn't see my left, and I knock his glasses off and he falls to the pavement. I cold cocked him, and I know he's out of it, but I also know when he comes around, there will be hell to pay.

So I get in the van and leave him in the parking lot like that. Like on all fours, shaking his head, like a bull that has been hit, but will be even worse when you get in the ring with him again. And yeah, my eye is blue already. He really caught me by surprise, but I caught him, too. The problem with a guy like Fernando is he'll never leave until he is sure there is no money he can get. And he really believes I owe him for being my dad. Like anything good I get should be his.

I'm thinking about Fernando so hard that I almost hit the blue car with the stubby antennas parked in our drive. The license plate has a star and I know right away this is not good. Mr. Jones is back.

20

YANKEE STADIUM. BABE RUTH comes up to bat. He had a bad season before, and this is the first game in the new stadium. A slow one comes in, and Ruth knocks it out of the park. Soon after that, they called Yankee Stadium the house that Ruth built. And now we are sitting in the house that Mom built, and this dude is talking to her and trying to take it all away.

"You are familiar with a Mr. Fernando Hernandez?" Mr. Jones is asking mom when I walk in.

Mom jumps up with her hair going wild.

"Ricky! What happened to your eye?'

"Ah, I caught a ball in my eye on a throw down."

The Pitcher his eyes narrow, and I know he isn't buying it.

"That is quite a shiner," Mr. Jones says with his coat off in a white shirt with a narrow tie. "Ha, ha."

'Yeah," I say. "Ha, ha."

But I'm really on fire, because didn't he just ask about Fernando? Mr. Jones has his briefcase open, and he is holding some file. He is sweating because Mom and the Pitcher don't like to run the air, and it's hot. I sit in another chair, and I wonder if they are deporting Mom. It doesn't matter; I will go with her. I made that decision a long time ago.

"Well. As I was saying, you do know a Mr. Fernando Hernandez?"

Mom glares at Mr. Jones like she will melt him with her eyes.

"Yeah, I know the asshole. He is my ex-husband."

"Ha, ha," Mr. Jones says, then nods

"I see. Well, Mr. Hernandez contacted our office and offered to testify against you. He basically says that you married Mr. Langford so you could continue living in the United States and—"

"That's bull," the Pitcher says.

"Oh, that asshole!!"

Mr. Jones is like turning red. Weird. Like he never heard anyone lose it. What white-people suburb is he from, anyway? He clears his throat several times and moves his hand through his hair. He probably sees Mexicans go crazy a lot. I mean, if somebody told me I had to leave after being here for thirty years, I would go crazy, too.

Mom is up now and pacing back and forth in her shorts with a shirt that says IMMIGRATION REFORM NOW. I mean, she holds these weekly meetings at our house where people make speeches and signs and get all riled up for demonstrations. Mr. Jones looks like he wants to run out the door.

Mom wheels around, her eyes sparking.

"I am going to kick his sorry ass."

Mr. Jones looks down at his file like Fernando is there somewhere. He purses his mouth and clears his throat several times and adjusts his skinny tie.

"Well, the problem is that we see a pattern here. It is one that you established with Mr. Hernandez of marrying people to provide you with citizenship and delaying deportation."

"Bullshit," Mom says standing in front of Mr. Jones. "The man is an asshole, but I never married him to stay here!"

Mr. Jones blinks looking like he's afraid to speak. But he does.

"Then why did you marry him?"

"Because I was pregnant, why else?" Mom shouts.

Mr. Jones nods slowly.

"Well, I wanted to get your side of it and make you aware of this development." He frowns. "Why would he come forth and say this after all these years."

"Take a look at the boy," the Pitcher says in a low voice.

Mr. Jones turns to me with this half smile on his face.

"'I'm sorry—"

"I said look at the boy."

I'm looking down now, feeling my face burning, man. I know where the Pitcher is going with this, and I don't want to go along with the ride. I look up at Mr. Jones, and he smiles stupidly

"That black-eye is Mr. Hernandez. He just smacked this kid, probably because he didn't give him any money," the Pitcher says slowly.

Amazing the way pitchers always nail it. I think good pitchers can read people's minds. I feel Mom's eyes boring in.

"Ricky! Is that true?'

"Of course it is," The Pitcher says, sitting back on the couch. He looks at Mr. Jones.

"This kid has a one-in-a-million arm, and he may play ball in the Majors, and this piece of trash has come back to extort money from him and his mother."'

Mr. Jones does the slow nod.

"Oh, that asshole!" Mom is now pacing like crazy. "I'm going to kill him, I swear to God I will!"

The Pitcher leans forward and pumps his finger at Mr. Jones.

"So, if that's someone you want to have in your file so you can throw my wife out of this country, then you better be damn sure he can stand up in court, because I will throw every lawyer I can hire at him."

Mr. Jones stares at the Pitcher like he just threw a fastball by his nose.

"I see," Mr. Jones murmurs. He shuts his briefcase. "Well, I still will need your written statement in about a week and half."

He looks at me and nods gravely.

"I am sorry for your troubles."

"Sure you are," the Pitcher says.

Mr. Jones then tries to look at my mom but thinks better of it and walks out the door quickly. Mom's eyes follow him, and then she watches him pull out of the drive. She turns around and faces me.

"Did Fernando do that to you, Ricky?"

I shrug and mumble.

"Yeah."

She turns to the Pitcher and says in a cool voice, "I'm going to kill him."

21

WALTER JOHNSON WAS ONE of the greatest pitchers ever, and he played with the Washington Senators. He went to the World Series against the Giants and in the seventh game held them off to the thirteenth inning. The Senators won, and Walter Johnson led the Victory Parade the next day to the White House. Calvin Coolidge met him there. The Washington Senators never won a championship again. And about right now, I feel like Walter Johnson and the White House is in the distance.

It's raining, and nobody is stopping the game. Not the coaches and not the ump. We are neck and neck, and I am up to bat and everything is slippery. The bat feels like it could just slide out of my hand like it did with Frankie when he swung hard on an inside fastball and the bat nearly hit the third base coach. I mean, it's not raining a little, it's coming down like sideways and the infield is mud soup and our shoes are sucking when we run the baselines and home plate is fast becoming a puddle. But nobody is calling the game.

It happens like that sometimes. You start a game, and then it clouds up and then the rain comes, but nobody thinks to call it because they think it will pass, or nobody sees lightning, or

somebody wants to win and get the call when they are ahead.
You never really know. Technically, it's up to the umps, but a
lot of times the coaches call the game, too. But we are neck and
neck bottom of the eighth, and I sure don't want the game called
because I have been really on.

I have been mowing them down with the old change up and
fastball, and Bailey has been riding the bench, which makes me
feel really good. And I had two triples and a double. Things are
looking up, and I'm thinking maybe my slump is over and this
Bailey guy will fade away and my grades will straighten up and
I'll graduate, and Mom won't get deported and the Pitcher will
bet a biopsy that will show his lungs are just fine and the MLB
scout will give me a contract. That's what's running through my
head when I go up to bat and face the Indians pitcher who has
been having a lot of trouble.

In fact, I'm amazed they haven't pulled him, because he looks
like one wet dog now. The water is dribbling off the brim of his
cap, and it's in the lights of the field and it's coming down even
harder now. Pitching in a rainstorm is about as bad as batting in
a rainstorm. The ball is heavy, and it slips out of your hand and
doesn't spin the way it's supposed too. And the bat feels heavy
and slippery. But the worst thing is the rain makes it hard to see
the ball.

You squint down toward the pitcher,, and all you see is lines.
And my eyes keep blurring. And this guy isn't hitting the zone
anyway, so I'm thinking I can just take his pitches and probably
walk. He's going into his set, and I really want to wipe my eyes
because they are blurry and I move the bat and wait, and usually
I can see the ball and track it as it comes in, but he comes forward
and it looks like a fastball, but I don't see it suddenly. Then I do
see it and it's right in front of me, and I don't have time to turn
away as I feel this sharp needle go right through my cheek, and
then it's lights out.

In my dream Mom is in the hospital, and I'm holding her
hand again. *Don't leave, Ricky,* she says. *Don't go.* I won't, Mom,
I say. We are barely hanging on again and don't have a penny
to our name, and Mom is real sick and looks like she's going to
die, and I'm telling her we won the game again and the Pitcher is
standing there with his head down and we are all really sad. But

then Mom is out of the bed, and now I'm in the bed, and she's holding my hand and telling me to come on back and that I have to wake up. And she is looking at me real worried the way she did a hundred times before whenever I had problems in school and the teachers told her I would never graduate and Mom was like, "No, he will graduate, and he will have his moment to shine," and she is telling me again I can do whatever I want. I just have to wake up and do it.

And I do, and she is by the bed with the Pitcher staring down at me, and they look terrible. Like they had just seen the worst thing in the world. And this doctor dude is looking in my eyes with a light, and these nurses are sticking me with all sorts of things, and Mom is crying like crazy now. They said I was out for like fifteen minutes, and now the room is moving, and it's like I can hear a siren, and I realize then we are inside an ambulance and the Pitcher is gone, or maybe he was never there, but the doctor or paramedic dude is talking to me.

"Hi, Ricky. Can you say hello?"

"Hello," I say.

I mean, I have one hell of a headache, and my cheek is pounding. And Mom's tears are falling on me, and she is cursing.

"Why didn't they call that game!"

Except she is cursing a blue streak, and I shut my eyes because the pain, man, is intense. And so I'm going to go back to sleep for a little bit. It turns out the baseball dented my cheek. Yeah. I now have a dent in my cheek and a concussion. They said they could reconstruct my cheek or could just let it go, and after a while nobody will notice. So I go with that and end up at home with painkillers after the Pitcher whistled in the hospital room and said, "Now that is a shiner." Yeah. I mean, I look like I was in some kind of a car wreck. My eyes are black and blue,, and my cheek is purple, and my face is swollen. The worst thing is I have to wear a mask now when I bat.

I look like the Phantom of the Opera dude.

Worse than all that, Bailey is now the pitcher.

22

BRANCH RICKEY STARTED THE farm system because he didn't want to have to pay for players. He decided to develop them. Soon he had eight hundred players in the system, and his team, the St. Louis Cardinals, started to win. Soon every team in the league adopted his system, and Minor League ball was born. Some guys moved up, and some guys didn't. You knew you weren't going to make it after a while. The way I knew I was out of it now and Bailey had taken my spot.

I took painkillers for three days. Vicodin. They put me up with the ceiling fan turning around and around. The whooshing noise of the fan became *whoosh, whoosh, whoosh.* I went into another world. Sometimes I just watched the fan and listened to it like the ocean. Then I was outside the Pitcher's garage all those years ago listening to his ballgames. A pitcher who won the World Series was in there, and all I had to do was talk to him and learn the secret. *The whole world is a full count against you, kid.* I knew what he meant, because I was watching Bailey Hutchinson talking to Jigger Hix.

Jigger is talking to and then sliding a check across the table. *But this is what the Chicago Cubs think about you.* It was

Moneyball all over, and Bailey is sitting there with his helmet on fire just burning up. Smoke is filling the room, and I can't see anyone anymore. Mom yells at me to put out the fire, but I can't. Christine sends me a text. *Breaking up with you. I am not going to prom.* Jigger Hix laughs loudly. *We all will be told when we can play the children's game anymore; we don't know when.*

I know I can't play the game anymore because the rain is coming down, and Mom and I are fighting with Fernando. He is coming for some money and he just hit Mom, and the Pitcher has his bat out and he and Fernando are fighting it out while Mom and I watch. There is nothing we can do about it, and Bailey is just burning them down on the mound. How could anyone pitch that fast? It was amazing. Maybe he was on steroids. But who could see for all the smoke? Now Es is yelling with her mouth moving and her head jiving.

"I would never go to prom with you if you were the last person on earth, Ricky Hernandez. You hurt me. You hurt me."

And now I 'm watching everyone graduate in blue gowns and caps, but there is one seat open, and Mom is crying and crying because I am not there. And I want to tell her I am sorry, because I feel so bad about not doing my schoolwork and making her do it and she is getting sick again and the Pitcher is laying in the hospital dying and Bailey Hutchinson just laughs and laughs.

This went on for three days.

23

GROVER CLEVELAND ALEXANDER WAS hungover and forty and playing for the St. Louis Cardinals after the Cubs let him go. They were down by two, and the bases were loaded against New York. The Cardinals coach called in Grover against their big hitter. Grover said he was going to pitch fast and inside, but Cardinals Manager Hornsby told him not to. Grover threw an inside curve, then an inside fastball. Then Grover went outside and struck him out. He kept the Yankees from scoring the next two innings and won the series.

I desperately need a win.

Mom and I are on the porch. I had quit taking the painkillers and come back to earth. We are sitting on the porch like we used to, and I'm still in my pajamas. Mom is smoking quietly, watching the Pitcher's old house across the street, where someone else had moved in. The garage had been dark, and then while we are sitting there, the garage lit up and the door went up a quarter. I stare at the light and Mom stares, and we both look at our own garage where the Pitcher had been watching a game. Neither of us said a word for a long time until Mom turns toward me.

"You know my dream used to be for you to make the high school team," she says.

"Yeah."

"But you did that, and then my dream became for you not to play baseball, Ricky. "

"Well, you got your dream," I mutter.

"No," Mom says. "Not this way."

I nod silently. Since I quit the painkillers, we had fought over my homework, and it had become like the old days. We hit each other with every fastball we could, and then we both cried. Mom couldn't understand why I wouldn't do my work to graduate, and neither did I. I really didn't. But every time I started, I fell asleep. I had already accepted that I wouldn't graduate.

Mom squints and stares at the Pitcher's old garage.

"My dream, Ricky, is to see you graduate. My dream is to see you in a cap and gown walk down the aisle with your other classmates and be able to decide what you want to do and have the world open to you."

She is staring at me, and I look down and nod. I mean, I feel real bad because Mom has gotten me through every single grade. I would have flunked out long ago if it wasn't for her. I couldn't even read in first grade, and Mom got *Hooked On Phonics* and we worked every night, and then I could read. I know I told you that before, but it's true. Everything I am, she is responsible for, and that includes baseball. So I feel like crawling underground because her eyes are wet again.

"Ricky. I didn't graduate high school."

And it's my turn to be shocked. I just stare at her, and she has this funny look, and I realize then she is embarrassed. And man, she should not be, you know. She has nothing to be embarrassed about. But I can tell she is.

"It's not a big deal, Mom," I say.

"Yes. Yes, it is a big deal. Graduating high school is an accomplishment. I dropped out because it was too hard and nobody could help me. But you have to graduate, Ricky. You have to do it for everyone in our family. You will be the first, and then you will go to college. That is my new dream for you."

I shake my head and look down.

"Mom, I don't know."

She nods like she used to nod about me making the baseball team.

"You will, Ricky. You can do anything you want if you believe you can. I know you might play baseball, but first you have to graduate college. I won't worry about you then."

Then she gets real quiet and leans forward and looks at me.

"Jack and I won't be around forever," she says quietly.

I stare at her.

"What do you mean?"

"I mean, I think Jack is sick, and Lupus doesn't go away. It goes into remission. My point is you must plan for the future now. You have to struggle to be the best you can be now, Ricky. I won't be around to push you along one day."

Now I am freaking. Mom is talking like she could die any minute, and the Pitcher hasn't sounded too good lately, and he still hasn't gone in for the biopsy. I look down, and Mom sits by me and rubs my shoulders.

"Remember how we used to do this? How after games we would sit together at McDonald's and Dairy Queen, and I would rub your shoulders because you were sore?"

I bite my lip and nod.

"Yeah, Mom."

I mean, I'm trying to keep it together because I feel like everything is slipping away. I lean against Mom, and I can feel how thin she is, and I don't want to think about her words, but I feel like she could just go away any minute.

"You're going to graduate, Ricky Hernandez, and be the first. You can do it."

"Yeah, I know, Mom," I say, wiping my eyes quickly.

We just sit there together on the porch and listen to the crickets and watch it get dark. Mom smokes, and the light under the garage glows like some kind of star from long ago.

24

TY COBB SAW BASEBALL as war. He ended up with a .367 batting average and almost beat a man to death who taunted him. The Pitcher and I are back in Redling Field, and I feel like we have just returned to a battlefield. It looks smaller to me now. The backstop seems like something for kids, and the bench is short and more faded. The baselines have faded, and the bases are just the metal rivets. Home plate is covered in sandy red dirt, and the fence is rusted. The trees are bigger, and I try and pick out the tree the Pitcher had me hit four years ago. There is a haze over the field, and a few birds sing in the trees as I walk up to the plate and look at the Pitcher with the mask on my face.

"Alright, let's just see how you treat this," he says.

It was his idea to go to the field and get me out of the house. I had hit a low funk because the local papers are all about Bailey Hutchinson, the new fireball from Texas. He won the last three games for South, and the coach and everybody had jumped on the shiny new Bailey wagon. I even wondered if he put the kid up to it who beaned me.

But right now I'm staring down the Pitcher as he winds up and slides one past my chin. And I flinch. I mean, I step back from the ball and want to crawl out of the batter's box.

"Yeah, that's what I figured," he says picking up another ball from a bucket.

It happens all the time. Guys get hit, and they are never the same. I didn't think it would happen to me, and I look for that other kid so cocky from before. He had it all against him then, too, but he didn't step back. The Pitcher throws another one in there, and I blink. It's like I can feel the ball hitting me, and I swing late. Three more come in the same way, and each time I feel this paralysis. I can't move for a second, and it's in that second that you have to swing. The Pitcher finishes with his bucket of balls and lights a cigarette.

He then walks in from the mound and guns a finger at me.

"We got a problem."

He says for me to go back to the plate. I go back and stand there while he sets himself again.

"Shut your eyes," he calls out.

"What?"

"Shut your eyes, rock-head."

I shut my eyes and hold the bat, which feels really weird.

"When I tell you to swing, then you swing. Got it?"

"Yeah."

"What!"

"Yeah," I shout.

I stand there in the dark with the bat on my shoulder. I can hear the birds and a plane and a dog and then a mower. Then I hear nothing but the whiz of the ball through the air.

"SWING!"

I swing and feel the ball go through the bat and open my eyes. The ball flies over the Pitcher's head. He holds up another ball.

"Shut your eyes again," he says.

I shut my eyes and wait. I can hear his windup and the creak of his glove and then the ball cutting the warm morning air. "SWING!" And then the ball connects again with the bat and takes off. We watch the pill land far out there in the outfield, and the Pitcher holds up another ball. We do this until Mom brings lunch. We sit in the field on a sheet and eat the fajitas out of tin foil. The Pitcher and Mom laugh and talk, and I sit eating silently, and we are a family again.

"After this, Ricky, you have homework," Mom says cleaning up lunch.

"Yeah. I know," I grumble.

The Pitcher sits quiet except when he coughs and hacks into the grass. Mom said he still hasn't gone to the doctor. When we finish eating, we go back to the field, except this time I pitch. I throw my fastball, a sinker, a curve and a changeup. The Pitcher stands slowly and nods slowly.

"You are ready for the Texan," is all he says.

25

DURING THE GREAT DEPRESSION most people couldn't afford the fifty cents to get in. Those that ate at the park made the five-cent hotdog their only meal for the day. Attendance fell off, and the National Past Time became endangered. Who cared about baseball when you were hungry or sick? Or when hard times had come back the same way Fernando has come back? There were just bigger problems. And now one of those bigger problems is banging on the door.

The moon is low, and it must be like three AM. The banging goes through the whole house, and then the doorbell is going off. *Ding Dong. Ding Dong. Ding Dong.* I am up and walking through the house, but the Pitcher cuts me off in his shorts and T-shirt, In his right hand is a Louisville Slugger.

"Go back to bed," he says.

But I follow him anyway. He pulls back the door just as Mom comes in putting on her robe. I look past him and see Fernando in the moonlight. He is weaving back and forth with his eyes red and glassy, and he smiles. Mom jumps in front of the Pitcher.

"Get out of here, Fernando, before I call the cops!"

He shrugs and holds his arms wide. He smiles real slowly.

"Hey, baby...you know I need a little spot, man, and figured you here with your big happy family man. Hey, bro, what is going on?" he says to me.

It's like he never hit me, and I never hit him. But I don't even want to look at him. One of the black eyes I have is from him, and I can feel my heart pounding away.

"I hear you got hit, man. You got to get better, you know, so I can get my payout, man," he says, nodding slowly.

"Get out of here," the Pitcher says stepping forward and raising the bat.

Fernando takes a step back. His eyes have narrowed and become small like a snake.

"Yeah, man. You messed me up real bad. It's why I got a cane now, man. You messed up my knee and my shoulder, but you ain't going to do that again, hombre."

The Pitcher raises up the bat higher.

"I'll do it again you don't get out of here."

Fernando reaches around behind him like a gunslinger and brings up the black pistol and points it at the Pitcher's nose. And nobody moves. Nobody breathes. You can hear time ticking in that moment. It's like we all became statues or something. My heart is pounding in my ears.

"Oh, really? So you the big man while you steal my woman and my kid. I ought to bust a cap on you right now for just doing that, man. "

He has the barrel almost touching the Pitcher's nose. The gun looks bigger now. Like it is a bazooka or something, and I'm staring at Fernando's finger curled around the trigger, and I am hearing that gun and seeing the Pitcher sprayed all over the door.

Mom's face is white in the moonlight, and I'm not breathing because Fernando is high and he might just shoot. The Pitcher nods real slowly, and his eyes never move, and he says in a voice cool as winter.

"You better shoot, rock-head, if you're going to pull it out."

Fernando nods.

"Don't worry about that, man...I'll shoot. I'll blow your head off!"

"Fernando, what do you want?" Mom says in this calm voice.

She knows he is crazy enough to shoot.

"Like I said, man, I just need a little spot. "

"Don't give it to him, Maria," the Pitcher says

"Give it to him, Mom," I shout.

And she goes back into the kitchen while we stand there like statues. Fernando still has the gun straight out, and I'm thinking, *Where are the cops when you need them?*

"Yeah, man. You there like superman. You going to take the cash when Ricky signs, right? I'm going to get my due, man. No way you going to screw me out of that."

"You ain't getting nothing, ya bum," the Pitcher says. "And you better put that peashooter away before you hurt someone. I seen guys like you all my life. You think the world owes you something, but it don't. All it owes you is a kick in the ass. You're just a bum."

Fernando steps up close with the gun an inch away from the Pitcher's head.

"Call me a bum one more time, and I'll blow your brains out, man."

Mom comes up then and holds out two hundred dollars,

"Here, now get out of here!"

"Good thing you came when you did, Maria, or I was going to take this old bitch out."

"Yeah. Sure you were, rock-head," the Pitcher says.

Fernando takes the money and lowers the gun. He's trying to act like the badass, but it's like he's a boy playing around a man.

"Yeah, man. You just got a couple hondos laying around. Life is good, huh, Maria?"

"Get out before I call the cops, Fernando!"

Fernando smiles.

"Nah, you won't call them, baby. Because that man at Immigration knows all about your sorry ass and how you really stayed here."

"Get out!"

"Yeah, get out, ya bum," the Pitcher says.

Fernando then looks at the Pitcher and snaps the barrel of the gun against his forehead. The Pitcher falls back with blood breaking a river down the side of his face. Fernando steps back and puts the gun back into his belt.

"I told you about calling me a bum again. You just be glad I didn't bust a cap on your ass."

Then he looks at me.

"You be careful with your arm, bro. "

And then he just walks down the sidewalk to his ghetto ride and slinks away like some kind of creature. The Pitcher is on the hallway floor, bleeding everywhere while Mom holds a dishtowel against his head. I watch the taillights car go down the street and vow to get Fernando one way or another.

26

ROBERT MOSES "LEFTY" GROVE was a savage competitor. He sometimes threw at his own teammates during practice, but he was one of the best pitchers the Philadelphia As ever had. He would smash his locker and rip his clothes when he lost a game. His tantrums became legend. Now I feel like smashing my locker and ripping my clothes because Christine has not shown up.

I wait and wait and call her cellphone and text her, and no Christine. Finally I drive Mom's old minivan to school, and I pull in and see Bailey's big black pickup with blond hair trailing out the passenger side like a flag. The flag says, *I won and took your girl, too.* I mean, who sells that kind of flag anyway to guys with flaming helmets from Texas? And they look like the All American couple, and I stand in the parking lot and feel really stupid, but I say it anyway.

"Hey, you were supposed to pick me up."

Christine stares at me.

"Didn't you get my text?"

"No!"

"Oh, well...I got another ride."

Christine just kind of laughs, and Bailey cracks a grin.

"She got a better ride, Mex, than in some ghetto van."

And then I'm running, and he drops his books or whatever he had, and we collide right there in the parking lot. And it is like flurry of fists, man. I mean I punching away, and he is punching away, and I feel my nose crack, and there is blood everywhere, and I'm not sure if it is from him or me, but I'm not stopping, and he's on the ground but putting up a good fight, and then somebody is dragging me back. He jumps up and lands the last punch.

My other eye.

And then there are people around us both and yelling and screaming, and we end up down in the principal's office and my nose is bleeding even with the towel I'm holding from the nurse. Mr. Drakotz, the principal, is staring at the two of us, and the Bailey guy's jaw is kind of blue, and he has a cut over his right eye.

Mr. Drakotz is like a vet from Iran with a Marine cut, and he looks mad.

"So what happened," he says.

I have my head back to stop the blood, and my T-shirt is done. It is a bloody mess.

"He attacked me for no reason," Bailey says.

"Bullshit," I say through the rag. "He called me a Mex."

Mr. Drakowitz, who has the smoothest head in the world, looks at Bailey.

"Did you call him a Mex?"

"Of course not. I have lots of Latino friends, sir. I would never do such a thing."

"Bull."

The principal turns to me.

"Is that why you attacked him then, Ricky?"

"Yeah," I answer.

Bailey scoffs.

"That's a lie."

Just then Coach Hoskins walks in and stands against the wall. He has on his South High shirt and looks tired.

"There are other reasons?" The principal wants to know.

Bailey stretches out his cowboy boots.

"Yeah. I beat him in pitching, and I took his girl. That's why he really hit me."

Mr. Drakowitz looks at me. I have come forward because the bleeding is slowing.

"Is that true, Ricky?"

I shake my head.

"No. He called me a Mex."

The principal nods slowly.

"Did he take your girl?'

I shrug and don't say anything. The principal looks up.

"Coach, do you want to add something?"

He comes off the wall.

"Yeah. I want both of you boys down in my office when Mr. Drakowitz is finished."

The principal shrugs. "You can take it from here. Any more fighting, and you are both going to be suspended."

So we follow coach down the through the school with me holding the towel to my nose. I have to listen to Bailey's boots click on the tile floor the whole way while Coach walks with his hands out. People stare at us as we go into the locker room and then into his glassed-in office. I sit in the chair, and Bailey slumps against the wall. I bring the towel down that is just all red. Coach throws me another one.

"Who is going to tell me what happened?"

Bailey tilts his head back and looks through slitted eyes.

"I told you, he attacked me for no reason."

Coach Hoskins, who is big and bald with hair rimming his ears and watery blue eyes, looks at me.

"Is that true?"

I shake my head.

"He called me a Mex."

"I don't know what you're talking about," Bailey says.

"You're a liar."

"That's enough!" Coach shouts.

Coach leans back and looks at the two of us.

"Why do I think this is over who gets to pitch?"

I don't say anything, and Bailey shifts his feet.

"I can't have you attacking people, Ricky, because they might be taking your spot."

I look up and feel the shock go down through me. Coach Hoskins takes this deep breath and looks at me.

"I wasn't going to tell you this, but I'm going to start Bailey the next game and see how he does. You can close it up for us."

And I know how this goes. Soon I will be in the outfield, and it just stings, man. It really stings. And I can feel Bailey's grin. He is wearing it like a sword he just plunged into my heart. I had been the starter for the last two years, and now in one week I have lost it all.

Coach looks at me.

"Do you have a problem with that?"

"Fine with me," Bailey sings out.

I look down for a long minute, and then it's like I am watching somebody else. This somebody else stands up and looks down at his baseball coach and says, "I quit."

Coach Hoskins eyes grow large.

"What!"

The coach's mouth opens and then shuts. He sputters.

"Think about what you are doing, Ricky."

I stare at him, and then somebody else replies again.

"I just did," he says standing and walking out.

That somebody else takes no shit from anybody. He is a scary dude.

27

SATCHEL PAIGE MAY HAVE been the greatest pitcher of all time. He called his fastball the *midnight rider*. His change-up was the *three-day creeper*. He liked to guarantee he would strike out the first nine men up, then call in the outfield and make good on his promise. Satchel did to black baseball what Ruth did to white baseball. He reinvented the game. Something I am doing right now, except it is not baseball.

Think of a courtroom, only it's not a courtroom, but a room with a long table, and around it are all your teachers. One guy sits at the head of the table, and you are sitting at the other end with your Mom, and everyone is staring at you like you just committed a crime, and your Mom is busy crying because these teachers are not your friends. They are ratting you out in a big way, and all you can do is sit there and listen, and the worst part of it is that they talk like you aren't there.

"Ricky will not apply himself. He sleeps during class and frequently looks out the window, and if I ask him if he has his homework done, he just shrugs."

That's my English teacher, Mrs. Warren. And this meeting is really about whether I'm going to graduate or not. I have had lots of these meetings over the years. They are my team. But with a team like this, who needs rivals, right? I mean, they are part of my Individual Education Program, and it is supposed to help me, but all I see is a bunch of people who just want to say what a bad student I am and how I could do better if I wanted to. And Mom just listens and glares at me.

"Ms. Hernandez, the reason we called this emergency meeting is because we are seriously concerned about Ricky's chance to graduate with the rest of the kids."

Pow! Mom just got one to the solar plexus. A real gut shot, because this has been her fear for four years. That I would not walk down the aisle with the other kids, and now Mr. Zimmer who is the school psychologist and team leader just laid it out there.

"And so we are going to go around the room and get status reports and name the areas that need emergency intervention. Mr. Thomas, would you like to go?"

Mom sits there in a dark blue dress and white blouse. She looks like a business lady. Mr. Thomas is my Sociology teacher and does not like me. He frowns at me.

"Ricky has not applied himself and has not turned in the last project. If he does not complete the project by the semester's end, then I will have no choice but to fail him."

And it's like he's the quarterback or something and all the rest are the ends, because they all catch his pass and start running like crazy.

"He does not work."

"He has the potential, but won't use it."

'I don't see how he can graduate."

"I wish he would not talk in class."

"He uses his phone in class."

"He is disruptive."

"I think he would rather be playing baseball."

"He doesn't seem to want to do better."

I mean, every teacher just lobs in a sinker. And it is like one-two-three. You try sitting in a room where everyone is criticizing you, and see how you like it. Every single one of these meetings goes like this, except this one is really bad because there is two weeks to the end of the year, and everyone is just throwing in the towel.

Except Mom.

When the room is quiet, she faces all of them at once and speaks in this low steady voice.

"Are you all finished?"

The teachers look around, and they kind of shrug.

Mom then stands up, and she goes real ethnic with the chin bob.

"How easy for all of you to say you don't see how Ricky can graduate," she cries out. "How about I hear a little about what we can do to get to graduate? You are supposed to be teachers. I don't see any teachers here, just a bunch of people whining about a student who won't act the way they want him to!"

"Mrs. Hernandez I don't think—"

Mom cuts off the case worker and points her finger at each teacher.

"You will email exactly what has to be completed for him to pass. Each of you. I will make sure the work is done. My son will graduate. My son will walk down that aisle with the rest of his class, and shame on each of you for not helping him to accomplish that!"

And just like that, Mom walks toward the door and I follow. And it has been like this for like four years. You would think Mom would give up on me by now. But she doesn't give up on anything. She would make a hell of a pitcher.

28

ERIC QUIT BASEBALL AFTER I beat him out for the pitcher. You remember Eric. His mom is still trying to get my mom deported. He went steroid after that and became a football player and started hanging around with the beefeaters. These are the muscle heads who pretty much hang in the weight room and listen to Metal and play football. Eric really chunked up and got tats and still keeps his hair in a razor crew. His blue eyes are even weirder now, and I think he looks like one of those dudes that would pull a Columbine.

We pretty much stayed clear of each other, so I thought it was really weird when he landed at the lunch table where I was eating by myself. A lot of times I hang with the baseball players, but today I just felt like being alone with my two black eyes. I had just come back to school, and everyone just stared at me, and I had to explain a hundred times I got hit with a fastball. I didn't bother explaining Fernando gave me the other black eye.

So when he hit the table and just stared at me, I felt a little weird. I had just opened my lunch and pulled out a cupcake. Remember what he did before? He stole my cupcake and held it in his mouth like he was going to eat it, and that's when I pulled the plastic knife, and that got me suspended. So these memories are lining up while Eric stares at me with this big grin and his eyes dancing.

'So I hear you quit the team," he says.

"Yeah," I say shrugging.

Eric frowns.

"Well, with that Bailey dude, I don't blame you. He smokes everybody. I heard he got a letter of intent from the Cubs," he says like he's just making conversation.

And just like that, he lands one. I mean, I am staring at him and he laughs.

"Oh, you didn't hear that, huh? I guess he is the real thing, not like that BS you were spreading around on Facebook."

And then I say something to him Mom will not let me print, you know.

Eric sits back and looks at me, and I know now why he sat down. Revenge is a dish best served cold, someone said, and Eric was serving it up ice cold.

"Man, you still got a mouth...Beano."

My heart is going *bam bam bam,* and I am back to fight or flight mode. Looks like I won't be in school that long after all.

"Get out of here," I tell him, giving him fair warning.

I mean, I didn't want to stare at his dancing eye and his big white teeth anymore. He looks down and sees my cupcake, and it's like instant replay. He picks up the cupcake and before I can say a word takes a big bite. I don't think I said anything, but the first punch knocked the cupcake out of his mouth. And then we both stood up, throwing punches like that super old game Rock'em Sock'em Robots. We both landed a couple before Mr. Truss, same dude as before, got between us, and then, like before, we went down to the principal where I explained that Eric took a bite of my cupcake and that's why I punched him in the mouth.

And like before, I got suspended for three days. When it rains, it pours, right? At least this time I could drive myself home.

29

BABE RUTH WAS SUSPENDED for six weeks in 1922 for
barnstorming in the off season. Then he was suspended two
more times for arguing with umpires, cursing, and throwing dirt
on them. He was at the top of his career. He didn't change and
continued drinking and womanizing. I am not the Babe, so I 'm
not sure how being suspended is going to go over.

The Pitcher is in the garage when I pull up.

I sit in the car and check out the raccoon in the rearview
mirror. That would be me. Fortunately, Eric just landed a couple
on my jaw that did nothing. I breathe heavy, glad Mom isn't
home. I walk into the garage, which is all the way open, which is
kind of weird. The Pitcher is standing and looking for something
on a shelf. The stitches from the other night look like railroad
tracks on his forehead. I asked him later how he knew Fernando
wouldn't shoot him, and he just shrugged and said he didn't.

He turns from the shelf and frowns at me.

"School out early or something?

"Yeah...or something."

The Pitcher puffs on a cigarette and squints.

"Yeah..."

"Yeah. I got suspended," I mutter.

The Pitcher nods slowly and shrugs.

"Good. I thought maybe you got in trouble or something."

I slump down in the La-Z-Boy and stare at the dark television.

"What'd they suspend you for?"

"Fighting."

"Hmmm." He sits down and cracks open a beer, then drinks. I am waiting for the other shoe to fall. He sets the beer down and gestures with his cigarette. "Oh...you going out for the boxing team?"

"Maybe."

"I mean, I figure since you aren't on the baseball team anymore and you like boxing so much."

He clicks on the television to a ballgame. It was a college game, and it meant nothing to me.

"The guy was an asshole."

"The world is full of assholes, so you better bone up on your right hook."

"Well, he was an asshole."

The Pitcher frowns again and stares at the game.

"That's good. I thought you punched him because he was such a nice guy. "

I rub the arm of the chair.

"He took a bite of my cupcake," I explain.

"Huh." He ashes his cigarette and picks up a puck of Skoal.

"Well, that's a good reason to get suspended for three days. "

"Yeah."

Shortstop groans on his side and looks up at a passing car.

"How can this Bailey kid pitch so fast?"

The Pitcher shrugs

"I dunno. Must have a fast arm."

'He pitches faster than me."

The Pitcher gestures behind him.

"And there's a guy over the next hill who throws a hundred. It don't mean nothing if you don't use the noodle. I told you that. Lot of fast pitchers out there."

I breathe heavy and close my eyes. The world feels like it's tilting away.

'He has a letter of intent from the Cubs."

"So what. That and a nickel won't even get you a cup of

coffee," The Pitcher grumbles.

"Still. It's something."

"Bull." The Pitcher spits into an old can. "He has a fast arm so they are keeping an eye on him, but that don't mean they are going to draft him. They want the whole package."

"Well, they don't want me now,"

"Yeah. Probably not after you quit."

I turn on him, feeling stung.

"I quit because they were going to play Bailey!"

The Pitcher ashes his cigarette on the floor

"Well, that's a hell of a good reason. Do you know how many times I would had to quit if I quit every time they played some Johnny come lately rock-head in my position?"

"No."

"Plenty, rock-head. There is always somebody after your spot. This kid got lucky and you got beaned, and then you quit. You played his gamed and not yours. After I told you a hundred times, you gotta play your own game."

I frown.

"What do you mean, he got lucky?"

The Pitcher swigs his beer and spits into a Skoal can.

"He comes in and fans you with some fast balls and you get the jitters, and then you get beaned and then you get mad and quit. Another guy would have never quit. He would have fought for his position instead of getting mad like some kid whose toy just got taken. "

I jump up in the chair.

"He's faster than me!"

"Yeah. That's what he wants you to think."

"You saw him! He pitchers faster and bats it out of the park every time!"

The Pitcher shrugs.

"Maybe he's on a streak; like you think you're in a slump, maybe he's on a hot streak"

I stare at him and start to feel like I had been played. The helmet with the flames. The pickup truck. The taunting "Mex." Taking Christine.

"The guy throws fricking fireballs. Nobody pitches like that," I mumble.

"Only one other guy I know. "

I stare at him.

"Who?"

The Pitcher leans back in his chair.

"Just a guy who used to pitch."

"What happened to him?"

The Pitcher stubs his cigarette, looking down.

"He got mad and quit because some guy conned him into thinking he had lost it."

I felt my face burning up now. "Yeah, what happened to him then?"

The Pitcher turns and looks me in the eye.

"Not a damn thing."

30

BABE RUTH CALLED HIS SHOT in Chicago. He was up and had two strikes, and then he just pointed to centerfield and then hit the longest home run ever seen in Chicago. Some people never believed he called it; others swear he did. When asked if he called it by a reporter, the Babe shrugged and said, "Well, you guys said I did, so it must be true." Like I said before, you either believe or you don't. Right now I don't believe in much, and maybe that's why the Pitcher woke me early the next day.

"Get up."

That's all the Pitcher said to me. I figured it was three days of snooze time, but Mom said it was three days of homework, and I was putting that off as long as possible. So when I opened my eyes and the Pitcher is standing by the bed with his old Tigers hat on and his glove and in some dirty ripped shorts from like 1925, I knew something was up.

"What?" I ask groggily.

"C'mon. Practice starts in ten minutes, and I ain't waiting all day for you."

I sit up and blink. I really want to go back to sleep.

"Hey man...I'm suspended... remember?"

The Pitcher looks down at me.

"Yeah. So I figure you got nothing better to do."

I shut my eyes and fall back.

"I'm tired," I mutter.

"And grab the rocks...rock-head."

I open my eyes again and stare at this crazy man.

'What!"

"You heard me, rock-head. Get the two buckets and put them in the back of my station wagon. "

I feel like this pinch between my eyes. I never wanted to throw those rocks again. I mean, a couple of times I had picked up the bucket just to remember what it was like...but no, I did not want to go back to those days.

"I am not throwing rocks again!"

He stares down at me and raises his eyebrows.

"You obviously didn't learn a damn thing the first time, so I figure we better start from the beginning again. Get the rocks."

I groan and fall back to my pillow.

"Oh."

"Yeah, ten minutes or you're walking."

And now we're back at Redling Field with the two buckets of rocks. Can you believe it? I can't. I mean, I never thought I would throw another rock again, but here we are. The Pitcher is smoking and hacking and spitting, and we are just outside the baseball field. The birds are singing, and the morning is on half the field and it's kind of peaceful and it's weird, because it doesn't feel like any time has passed. The Pitcher looks at me.

"So," I say.

He gestures to the dirty white buckets.

"So pick up a rock."

I look down at the squat buckets piled high with rocks.

"This is so stupid," I mutter.

He pipes up a cigarette and stares at me.

"Oh, yeah. Getting suspended is stupid. Getting in fights is stupid. Quitting your team is stupid. So I think you should be real comfortable with stupid things like throwing rocks."

"Almost as stupid as smoking when you might have cancer."

"Almost."

I swear and shake my head and pick up a rock.

"Alright, let's see you hit that tree."

I stare at him and frown and then stand up. My mouth drops open, and I look across the field. That same tree is there from three years before. I mean this was really all a bad dream.

"Wait a minute, you don't mean. You don't mean that—"

"That's right, rock-head. Yeah, the one you could never hit before."

I stare across the field at the tree that is bigger now, but still looks like it's a million miles away.

"Go ahead. I'll bet you still can't hit it."

I close my eyes. My life was getting weirder every minute. One minute, I am the man on the baseball team, and now I'm back to trying to hit a tree with a rock.

"Alright."

I pick up a flat one and hold it lightly in my hand. I look at the Pitcher, but he just motions across the field. "Go on. I'll bet that Bailey kid could hit it."

"My ass," I say. Now I'm pissed.

I draw back and let fly and, of course, I throw wide. The Pitcher looks at me.

"Yeah. Some things never change. You just can't hit a tree with a rock, can you, rock-head?"

I throw five more rocks and don't even come close.

"Alright. Let's see you hit it."

The Pitcher stares at me, then turns and stares at the tree. He shuts one eye and seems like he's measuring the distance or something. He turns to me.

"I hit it, then you run around this field three times."

"Sure. You're on."

I hate running, but I know he is not going to hit it. I mean, the Pitcher just isn't what he was three years ago. He picks up a rock from the bucket and squints at the tree. He puts his cigarette in his mouth and leans back. He pauses and takes a breath, then throws the rock. It arcs up high like a black dot and then sails down and pings against the tree with a crack that goes across the park. The Pitcher takes the cigarette from his mouth and gestures across the field.

"How in the hell did you hit that?" I cry out.

"Because I know how to pitch. Now get running, rock-head."

Yeah, I still hate running. And every time the Pitcher hits the tree or the backstop or a sign or a bird or a plane, I have to run. And it's hot. And we keep at it for the next three days, because the Pitcher says I have forgotten everything he had taught me and so we are starting over from scratch. Every time I finish the bucket, the Pitcher just nods like he did all those years before and says three words:

"Get the rocks. "

God. I hate those rocks.

31

IN THE GREAT DEPRESSION men thumbed their way to Florida to try out for the Major Leagues. They were not after stardom; they were after a job. Some collapsed on the field from exhaustion and starvation. Few made the team. I was like those guys now with few options, and it was like I was trying to make the team all over again. So for the next three days, this old World Series pitcher and this really pissed-off Hispanic teenager went to Redling Field every day.

We get there and the Pitcher always tells me to run like before, and I bitch like before, and then we get down to business with the rocks. But this time, the Pitcher adds a few things. Sometimes he throws a rock across the field and then turns to me.

"Go find it," he says.

I stare at him still squinting against the morning sun.

"What are you, crazy?"

The Pitcher looks at me with these dull eyes.

"Look, you want to get your spot back from this Texan Bailey kid, or don't ya?"

"Well...yeah, but I don't see—"

"Shut up and go find the rock."

Then he just watches me a while, I fume and stomp across the field and start looking. I look for an hour, and I can't find the rock or I bring back a different rock. I figure he won't know the difference.

"That ain't my rock," the Pitcher says in the shade, having a cold Good Times and smoking a cigarette and having some Skoal and hacking his guts out. I mean, he hacks and hacks and hacks. I stare at him and shake my head.

"You ought to see a doctor, you know."

"I ought to do a lot of things."

And so I keep hunting for the rocks. Then he has me throw and throw and throw. Then he gives me a baseball and tells me to bring the heat. I throw it as hard as I can against the backstop with the ringing off the fence like a church bell in the middle of the day. And then he sits on the bench and smokes like he used to before. He just stares at the field and then turns to me.

"You only got one shot, you know that, right?"

"Yeah."

"You got one life, and then it's just over. One day you're in front of the whole world, and then you are some guy sitting in his garage. You get that, right?"

"Yeah."

"Don't blow your shot."

"I won't."

"You sure?"

"Yeah."

"Alright, now go find the rocks."

We go back to throwing rocks or me throwing every kind of pitch in the world until my arm is on fire. And the Pitcher tells me about all the guys he struck out and how having a fastball is nothing if you didn't use your brain.

"I told you that before, right? You remember?"

"I know."

"Oh, yeah. But you forgot."

"Yeah."

"You remember the whole world is a full count against you?"

"Yeah."

"You remember you got to pick a spot?"

"Yeah."

"You remember it's your game?"

"Yeah."

"Then what happened?"

"I forgot."

"Do you do drugs?"

"No."

"Maybe you should start."

And then Mom brings us lunch like before, and we sit in the shade and eat. And I listen to her and the Pitcher talking like before. I shut my eyes and wonder what the rest of the world is doing and how the team is doing and how I lost my position. I wonder what Bailey is doing. Then I wonder about Christine and Es, and I feel bad about treating Es like I did, and I kind of want to call her, and then I think about Fernando who pulls up in his car and watches sometimes and then just drives away.

I think about all these things during these crazy three days, and then the Pitcher shows me something new. I mean, he hasn't shown me a new pitch in three years. So he calls me to the mound and holds out the ball.

"You ever heard of a forkball?"

I stare at him.

"No."

The Pitcher pulls on his cigarette. "Guy named Joe Bush of the Red Sox came up with it after World War I. Maybe he got gassed or something because it a weird pitch. I only used it a couple times because it tears up your arm. A lot of guys' shoulders blow out from this thing. "

He holds up the ball and positions his fingers.

"You open your two fingers like a fork. You jam the ball down in there and throw it just like a fastball but at the release point you snap your wrist downward like this."

I stare at him.

"So what's it do?"

The Pitcher shrugs.

"All sorts of crazy things. The biggest thing is it tumbles, then drops off the plate when it reaches the catcher's mitt. It's almost impossible to predict where it's going to end up. You don't know, and the batters don't know either. But like I said, you throw it like a fastball and sort of twist your wrist down at the end."

He hands me the ball and spits off the mound.

"Figure you could use something new if you get in a pinch with the Texan."

32

A LOT OF BASEBALL players didn't finish high school. The old players were mostly farm boys who either played ball or worked in the fields. You didn't need a high school education to hit a homerun or throw a spitball. So I am right in there. I have five semester projects due at the end of the week. And worse, I don't want to do them and don't know how to do them. I fall asleep, and Mom is trying to do my Econ project, complete with a PowerPoint presentation, and my English paper about a conflict I had last summer, and I'm supposed to study Biology and take a test that is really on the whole semester. And History. Yeah, the origins of World War II. It's not that I don't want to do my homework; it's that I really don't know how.

So I sleep. And sleep. And sleep. Whenever Mom and I sit down, I get sleepy, and it doesn't matter how many times I go to Starbucks or how many milkshakes she makes me or how many candy bars I eat or how many times I take short naps. I still want to sleep when it comes to my homework. It's like the thought of all that work makes me sleepy. Mom says it's because I am overwhelmed, and sleep lets me escape.

"You will not graduate, Ricky, if you don't do this," Mom screams.

"I don't care," I scream back. "I'm screwed anyway."

"What do you mean?" she screams.

"I mean I can't play baseball, and I can't graduate, and I am screwed!" I yell.

Mom's eyes go crazy.

"Don't say that!" She yells back.

"Why not? It's true," I shout back.

"You are just lazy, Ricky." She shouts.

"I AM NOT LAZY!" I scream.

Mom whips out her finger and points down at me.

"Yes, you are! It's why you quit the team. You would have to work to get your starting position back, and you are too lazy to even do that!"

So now I am bleeding. Mom knows just where to put the knife.

"Don't even go there," I say.

Mom shrugs.

"Why not? It's true!"

So I throw one right at her head. Not a brush back. A beanball.

"Yeah, and it's true they are going to kick your sorry ass out of the country. At least I know where I was born."

Mom's eyes get real big, and she comes at me.

"Don't you talk that way to me, you little shit!"

My turn to shrug.

"Why not? You lied your way in here and are probably going to screw it up for me!"

And then Mom tries to slap me, and I duck and run outside. I jump in the van, and Mom comes outside and screams to open the door.

I point to my ears and put it in reverse and leave her in the drive. I drive around until it is late and then come back and go to sleep until the Pitcher wakes me up and we go to the ball field and throw rocks. This is my life now.

"I'm tired of throwing these rocks."

"Why…you got something better to do?"

"Yeah, plenty."

"Well, I know you ain't doing your homework."

I stare at the Pitcher.

"So you talked to Mom."

"Yeah, we're married. Married people talk."

"And so what did she say?"

The Pitcher shrugged and coughed and spat in the grass.

"Just that you won't do your work, and all her work and time with you is a waste because you won't even help yourself. Other than that, not much."

I squint.

"She said that?"

"No. I did."

I scowled.

"Oh, listen to the guy who keeps smoking even though he has cancer."

The Pitcher looks down at me.

"Nobody said that, but even if I do, it's my business—and by the way, we ain't talking about me; we are talking about you. I already climbed the mountain. I pitched twenty-five years in the Majors and won a World Series. What have you done?"

"And you didn't have to graduate high school to do it," I point out.

"Those were different times then, rock head."

I shrug and look around the ball field to where some guy is walking his dog on the far side.

"So what. I can do the same thing."

"No. Just one small problem. You quit the team, remember?"

I shake my head. 'They know I'm good."

"Bull. All they know is that you are a quitter."

Man, did that sting. So I take the bucket of rocks and throw it across the field. The Pitcher calmly pulls on his cigarette

"Oh, good. Now you can go get the rocks, rock-head."

"NO! Screw this! I'm done."

The Pitcher stares at me and nods slowly

'Yeah, I think you are done, too, quitter."

Everything is backing up on me now. Being suspended. Quitting the team. Christine dumping me. And now the Pitcher riding me.

"Screw you. I don't need you. I don't need anybody," I shout marching across the field.

I reach the far end of the field and realize I couldn't go home because Mom is waiting with my homework. I stand around and kick the grass and cuss and then walk back across the field. The Pitcher is sitting down on the bench, watching me.

"Oh, the quitter is back."

I don't say anything. The Pitcher leans back and hacks out something in the grass, then nods to me.

"What are you waiting for?'

I look at him. He gestures to the bucket laying on its side.

"Go get the rocks, rock-head."

So I do.

Dasi Vance was a Brooklyn Dodgers pitcher. He literally had a trick up his sleeve. He bleached his sleeve to fake out the batter and confuse it with the ball. It worked, but the Dodgers rarely rose up above sixth place. Even their diehard fans called them *Damn Bums* in the beginning. Then they began to win, and they were just the Bums. I can relate because I am that damn bum now.

Mom and I have it out again. I'm crashed out in the basement, and she goes ballistic because I left a Panda Express bowl on the lawn. I hear this voice above me from the sanctuary of my covers.

"Is this yours, Ricky?"

I groan.

"What?"

"Is this yours?"

I look up and see angry Mom eyes. You don't want to see those when you first wake up. She is holding a black bowl like she's going to throw it at me or something.

"I dunno," I mumble.

Mom's eyes are doing double time, and she holds the bowl over my head.

"This was on the lawn. Is that what you think of our house?

A garbage dump!"

"Chill out, Mom. It's just a bowl."

Mom does not chill out. She goes more nuts and throws the bowl against the wall. Now I'm awake.

"It's bad enough you quit the team and are suspended for fighting, but you won't even do your homework so you can graduate, and this is how you treat me!"

I can't even wake up anymore without somebody riding me.

"What are you talking about? It's a bowl," I shout.

"I'm talking about you, Ricky! You are a jerk!"

I'm up now. I'm really up.

"Hey, you want me to move out, then say the word!"

Mom stares at me like I just swore at her.

"Where are you going to move, Ricky?"

"Anywhere but this shithole," I shout.

Really, I have no idea where I will move, but I have to fight with something, and Mom holds all the cards.

"Fine! Get out then! Fine, move out with no high school diploma; you will get real far!"

"It worked for your dumbass," I say, and then Mom comes at me.

I go under the covers and can feel her hands trying to find me. I fall off the couch and scramble away.

"I don t need a diploma," I shout going upstairs and grabbing my keys and my wallet.

I mean, I 'm still in my pajamas, but you can't pick your battles, you know. Mom is in the doorway when I come down.

She crosses her arms.

"Don't you take my car."

"Fine!"

I throw the keys and stomp out the door. I'm on foot. Could things get any worse? Oh, yeah. Es is walking toward me. She is not someone I want to see right now, but she has drawn a bead and is walking me down. And like I said, I am in my pajamas outside.

"Oh, so it's Mr. Asshole," she says.

"Hey, Es."

Her bright red lips start moving, and her head starts going like a parrot.

"So I heard you quit the team."

"Yeah."

"And that stuck-up rich bitch dumped your sorry ass."

"Yeah."

"And I heard you might not even graduate."

"That's right."

The parrot head goes back and forth and then sideways.

"You know what your problem is, Ricky?"

"No."

Es taps my head.

"Your head is too big. You think you are the hot shit guy, and now look what happened to you. You are nothing."

"Yeah. Okay."

"You shit all over people, and now you are getting shit on."

"Yeah."

I pause, thinking now is a good time as any to ask her to prom again. I mean, I'm really nuts when you get down to it. I just do things, and I don't know why. Would you ask a girl to prom who you dumped and you are now standing outside in front of in your pajamas while she is ripping on you? No. But I would.

"Hey, Es, you want to go to prom?"

The parrots head goes berserk. Her eyes start jumping, and her head goes back and forth.

"I wouldn't go with you if you were the last guy on earth!"

And then Es pushes me off the sidewalk and keeps going in her spiky heels. I turn back home. I mean really. Where was I going to go anyway?

34

IN THE BLACK LEAGUES pitchers were expected to go nine innings and would often hide a bottle cap in their glove to scuff up the ball to make it break more sharply. Spitballs, shine balls, nobody knew what the ball would do. Like nobody knows what I am going to do. I don't even know what I am going to do. Just like a spitball, I am off balance now, and it's anybody's guess where I will end up.

So I have this dream. Mom and I are back in the street, playing ball. It is before the Pitcher, and we are about to lose our home, and Mom is sick, and everything basically sucks. And Mom is trying to show me how to pitch again, and I'm throwing it all over the place. But here is the weird thing. I'm happy. I mean, I still haven't made the team, and you would think with everything against me that I would be depressed or something. But Mom is telling me again I can do whatever I want. And I believe her then, but somehow I have forgotten what she said. I don't really believe I can do whatever I want.

I just don't. Not the way things are now.

The rocks. The rocks are in the bucket. I throw the rocks. I pick up the rocks one at a time. I hate the rocks. It's like I am a prisoner and all there are are the rocks. The Pitcher just watches and smokes and drinks. I ask him if Mom knows how much he smokes and drinks. My game, he says. That's true. We work on the forkball then. I really can't get it to drop. The worst thing is I can't focus on what I'm doing.

"So what's the problem?"

That's the Pitcher, and I am throwing all over the place. The problem is Facebook and a letter of intent. Bailey put all over Facebook he is going to sign with the Cubs. I mean, that is my dream, not his, and he stole it, man. Just stole it from right under my nose.

"That's bull," the Pitcher says shaking his head

"It's on Facebook," I tell him.

"Well, that proves it's bull then."

Then Mom drops the big one. She says it doesn't matter if I go back to school since I won't try anyway, and it is a waste of time. So I might as well start looking for a job. So I call her bluff and end up at McDonald's the next day with a headset. Mom says I might as well get used to minimum wage jobs, because that is all I will have. I count the change and take the orders. Es comes through a bunch of times and makes a point of ordering a Diet Coke and acting like she doesn't know me.

It's busy at McDonald's, and I'm working the drive through. It's not so bad, but you have to do a lot of things at once like take the order and count change and sometimes give out the food. But tonight the cars are backed up, and I have one eye on the monitor, where you can see who is ordering. And I see this jacked-up F150 pickup round the curb, and this dude with a cowboy hat lean out, and I feel my brain pop and I am hot all over.

"Yeah, man. Give me three chipotle wraps with barbeque sauce on the side and a large Coke."

It is the Texas Bailey voice right in my ear ,and I give the next guy the wrong change. I mean I cannot concentrate, and my hands are shaking.

"Any ketchup?" I ask, keeping an eye on the screen.

"No, man. Just barbecue sauce," Bailey says with this stupid country music playing in the background.

"Yes, sir. That'll be six fifty," I say, disguising my voice.

And then I see myself in my hat and my McDonald's shirt, and I want to be anywhere but where I am. The F150 comes around the corner, and the Country Western is blaring from the cab as Bailey pulls up and he is like all hat. It is a big black hat that is low on two glimmering pieces of coal. That's what his eyes look like to me. Black coal.

"Six-fifty, sir," I mutter, keeping my head down.

He hands me a twenty, and I make change, and I can feel his eyes crawling over me. Then the grin. That grin says he has placed me somehow, but I 'm not surprised. All pitchers know about each other. It's like a club, and you always hear about who is good or who is fast. I hand him his change.

"Well, I wondered what happened to you. Guess you ended up where you belong, huh?"

I don't say anything but keep my head down.

"Well, thanks, Mex. Come around sometime, and I'll get you some tickets to the game. "

I look up at him then, and he just grins, then guns the truck away. I am totally off now and not hearing the guy over the headset, who is ordering about ten things. I am staring at the last order, and I consider grabbing Bailey's Coke and taking a piss in it or throwing his chipotle wraps in the trash. *Thanks, Mex.* It's Eric Payne all over again, and I cannot focus. *Thanks, Mex.*

"Hey, Ricky, man, the cars are all messed up. Here, go to the order window, man," Alfonso my manager says, taking the headset.

I give it to him, and he's right. My brain is fried. I cannot focus in on what anyone is saying. It's like I am all the way back four years before and Eric is calling me a beano and taking my cupcake.

"Hey, Ricky, take these Chipotle wraps and the Coke to the dude in the pickup truck," Julie my other manager says, handing me the bag.

"I really don't want to do that," I say.

She stares at me as if I have lost my mind. I mean, we are backed up, and in McDonald's, man, you never say no to a request.

"Just do it, Ricky," she says jamming the bag in my hands.

And now I have Bailey's two Chipotle wraps with extra barbecue sauce, and I am walking out the door. The black F150 is pumping out exhaust and country music, and I can see the DON'T TREAD ON ME sticker and the Confederate flag on the bumper. I can see Bailey's arm on the door, and a cigarette flicks into the dusk light. I think about just throwing his food away and going back in. But I know that will get me fired, and I need the job.

So I walk up to the window, and Bailey turns with that shit-eating grin.

"They got you doing everything, huh, Mex?'"

"*Si, Senor*," I say handing him the chipotle wraps.

And then just as I am handing him the Coke, I know what I am going to do. It's like the most natural thing in the world. I take the large Coke and pop the lid off and hand it to him. Just as he goes to take it, I turn it upside down and pour all that Coke in his lap.

He screams.

"You little bastard!"

"Oh, I am so sorry, *Senor*," I say, shaking my head. "My bad, *Senor*. I will get you another."

Bailey is out of his truck in his cowboy boots, trying to get that large coke off his pants, but it looks like he pissed down his leg. Then he is trying to get the Coke out of his truck, then whips around and grabs me by the shirt.

"You did that on purpose!"

I am praying he will take a punch, and I'll get him arrested then.

"Oh, no, *Senor*. It was an accident. I assure you."

"What's going on here?'

Alfonso is out in the drive with his headset.

"This fricking Mexican just dumped Coke inside my truck and all over me!"

Alfonso is a big dude, and he sees the truck and the stickers.

"There is no need for racial slurs, sir. I am sure it was an accident."

I am smiling at Bailey like the happy Mexican. He looks at Alfonso, then me and nods slowly.

"I get it. Screw the gringo. I'm just glad I wiped your ass off that mound, Mex, and I'll do it again."

And then he gets back in his truck and roars away.

Alfonso stares at him with the headset winking angrily on his head.

"You know that dude?"

I shrug.

"No. Never saw him before."

35

DIZZY DEAN WAS A cocky right-handed Pitcher for the Cardinals. A farm boy who had dropped out of school in the second grade. He was a cotton picker when Branch Ricky discovered him. He would often ask a batter, son, what kind of pitch would you like to miss? In the World Series he was hit in the head by a throw from the shortstop and knocked out. Headlines the next day said X-rays of Dean's head showed nothing. Lately, I could have had that same X-ray.

Joey picks me up after work, and we go cruising in his low-riding Chevy. He dropped out of school a while ago and has worked all over the place, but he has a lot of cash and I figure he is dealing, because he's started hanging with some gangbangers. He is slouched way down and pulls on some beer in a paper bag that doesn't taste so bad because it is a hot night, and after the thing with Bailey, I wouldn't mind getting a little fuzzed out, you know. I don't smoke weed because it slows me down, but I have had a few beers with the Pitcher in the garage, and so I hand Joey back the bag after taking a couple heavy pulls.

"Yeah, I know about your homeboy, Bailey," he says rubbing his goatee.

I look at him. "Yeah.'

"Yeah, man." He nods. "Don't you know, bro? He is all *roided* up. Got it from some dudes who supply him and who I supply.'

"No shit."

"Yeah, man." Joey drives cocked down with his hat on backward, wheeling the car around the parking lot. "You think he can pitch like that without some heavy-duty chemicals? Shit. I did some checking, you know. It's why they moved from Texas, man. He got kicked out of his school. He likes his blow, and he is heavy with cash. My man says he always has like a thousand bucks on him, which makes me think he is dealing

I look at him

"How's he know that?"

Joey shrugs.

"Because he gets him his drugs, man."

We drive in silence. Joey has been thrown out of his house a couple times and stays with his old man across town. He stops and parks in front of the old Pitcher's house. Some family bought the place, and the garage is all the way down. He looks across at our house with the garage up a little way and the light on. When he turns off the car, we can hear the ballgame.

"Shit...he was over there, and now he is your house."

I nod. "Yeah. Crazy, huh?"

Joey strikes a cigarette and shrugs, slumping down. It's been a long time since we hung together. It's like I went one way and he went the other, and in a way it's kind of sad, but I don't think about it too much.

"I remember how we used to throw all that shit under the garage. You remember that?"

"Yeah, man. Good times," I say, nodding.

Joey stares down the street then looks at me.

"So you going to play in the majors or what?"

"I don't know, man. I quit the team, you know."

Joey stares at me. "What do you mean?'

"I quit the team, man. Coach started playing this Bailey dude, and I just said screw it."

Joey shakes his head slowly.

"What are you doing, man? You got it going on. You got something, man. I am doing my shit because I don't have it going on...but you. Ever since we were kids, you had an arm, and now you can go all the way, man. You can't quit. You can't let some dude from Texas knock you off your thing."

Joey ashes his cigarette out the window.

"You're going to play, man. Nobody has an arm like you."

"That Bailey does," I grumble.

Joey frowns.

"That dude is all roids man. He ain't the real thing, but you are. You got it, man, and you just gotta suck it up, you know, and go kick his ass."

I shake my head.

"The MLB doesn't know that, man. They just see his fastball."

Joey looks at me in the half-light.

"You are the real thing, man. That dude's going to flame out."

I stare at Shortstop, who has just come out of the garage. He is real old now and moves pretty slow.

"I dunno. Lot of guys get called up and then just choke, man. Or they put you in the Minors, man, and you never get called up."

"Now you're talking shit."

"Yeah, well, I got smoked."

Joey stares at me.

"So what, man? Everybody gets smoked, but you don't lay down then, man. You fight back! That dude was all lit up on blow and roids. 'Course he smoked your ass."

I stare down our street and nod slowly. For the first time I feel like going back.

"Well, it doesn't make it any easier," I mutter.

Joey flicked his cigarette into the street.

"Nothing is easy, man. Nothing is easy. Look, man. You just keep playing the way you been for the last three years. They know who is the real thing, and they know who is bullshit. It's like their job to know the difference, you know."

"Yeah. Maybe," I mumble.

"So what up with this stuck-up bitch, man, you dumped Es for?"

I look at Joey. He always liked Esmeralda, and I know it burns him that I dumped her.

"I dunno, man. I just want to see what the other side is like, you know. Doesn't matter she dumped me."

Joey shakes his head.

"Damn, rich white chicks are going to dump the Mexican every time. You should know that, bro."

Joey taps the steering wheel and lights a cigarette. "You shouldn't ought to do Es that way, man. She really wanted to go to prom, you know."

"You take her, man."

He rubs his goatee, then smoothes his shaved head with his palm.

"You know she don't want nothing to do with me, man. Never has. It is your ass she wants. She always has ever since we were kids. You know that." Joey's eyes glimmer in the darkness, and he taps his cigarette toward me.

"You gotta remember where you came from, Ricky, even when you leave, you know."

"Well, I ain't going anywhere now," I say tiredly.

"Yeah. I hear about all these college dudes flying you all over the place."

"That was before. Besides, I got to graduate first, man.

"Uh-huh. You going to graduate."

I slump down and can see the Pitcher's ankles in our garage.

"Maybe not. I got like three classes borderline. Might just end up hanging at McDonald's."

"What! Get out of here, man," Joey says shaking his head. "You just feeling sorry for yourself. You got to graduate. Maria kick your ass all over the place if you don't."

I see Mom looking out the window just then.

"Yeah, I better go."

I get out of the car, and Joey leans over.

"Hear your dad is back, man."

"Yeah, the asshole is back," I say nodding.

"What's he want?"

I shrug.

"Figures I owe him if I go MLB."

Joey rests his hand on the steering wheel.

"He never did shit but beat your ass."

""I know. Tell him that."

Joey nods slowly, then looks up.

"You want some of my homies to have a word with him?"

I lean on his car and shake my head.

"It's cool. I'll handle him."

"Don't let him hit you, man."

"I'll kick his ass," I say

Joey looks at me again.

"Don't let this Bailey dude mess you up, man. You got a talent, man, you got an arm. You can't let this steroid dude knock you off, you know. You got something people will kill for, man, and you got an old man who can tell you what to do with it, and you got a mom who will do anything so you can get your dream. She is just busting your balls, man. She wants you to do the right thing, you know."

I hang on the window and nod. Joey stares at me.

"Don't end up like me, man. This is nothing, bro. But you got it, and you can't turn your back on your talent. It goes with having it, man. You ain't no McDonald's dude without a diploma. You are Ricky Hernandez with a million-dollar arm. You can't let down your mom or the Pitcher, man. They believe in you, you know. And so do I."

He leans over and nods, and we bump knuckles.

"You can't let down yourself, either, bro. "

Joey starts his car.

"Alright, man. I'll catch up with you," he says.

"Cool," I say.

He drives off, and for a moment it feels like old times with just the ballgame and the darkness and Shortstop asleep. I turn and stare at the house the Pitcher lived in. Sometimes, man, you just don't want the old times to end—even if they were bad.

36

CARL HUBBLE WAS A dominating screwball pitcher. He pitched so many screwballs, his arm was deformed with his palm facing permanently out. I feel like Carl facing my coach, like I am deformed or at least defective. He came over on Sunday night and says he wants to talk. We all sit in the living room. The Pitcher, Mom and me. Coach looks funny in his South High School shirt and big thighs in his shorts. He sits on the edge of the couch with his legs apart. He looks at me.

"I want you back. But I wanted to let you know, Ricky, that I am having trouble getting around the eligibility requirement."

Basically, he is talking about my grades. The teachers send these reports to the coaches that say how you are doing. And I am not doing so well.

"Ok," I say.

"Ok," Mom says

"Ok," the Pitcher says.

Coach rolls his hands and looks at Mom, then me.

"But I need your word that you will graduate. That you will do the work required and graduate. If I can tell the District that, then you are back on the team."

Like he is playing this all like I quit because of my grades or something. Maybe it lets us all save face in a way. Maybe Coach jumped the gun, too. Coach is looking at me, and then Mom is looking at me. The Pitcher is looking at me. I am looking at me. Can I do it? Can I graduate? I look at Mom, and her eyes are taking me apart. I nod slowly.

"Yeah. I will graduate," I say.

"He will graduate," Mom says.

"He will graduate," the Pitcher says.

The coach smiles and stands up.

"Alright. I will see you at practice tomorrow then."

He pauses.

"Bailey will be starting, but that is because you have been gone," he says in a way that shows he isn't happy about things either.

I look at Coach Hoskins. He has always been square with me, and I see how my quitting bothered him.

"I get it," I say.

He looks at me.

"You are still my main guy, Ricky."

I smile.

"Thanks, Coach."

Coach leaves happy. Mom turns to me, and her eyes are kind of glassy. The Pitcher looks different, too, and I don't want to use the word *respect,* but there is something in his eyes.

"Let's get to work," Mom says.

"Yeah, let's get to work," the Pitcher says.

"Yeah," I say. "Let's do it."

37

BABE RUTH WAS TRADED to Boston with the promise he would manage. He never did get the call to manage. His talent was leaving him, and his final homerun, number *714,* went out of the park and just kept going. He was forty and finished. But he went out on top. And maybe that is the thing. If you are going to go out, you want to go out on your own terms. And quitting was not my terms, and letting Bailey beat me was not my terms either.

So I am watching Bailey. He's been getting dressed for practice, and I'm by my locker. He looks up and cocks this big grin like he's Babe Ruth or something.

"So they are going to let you play even with your crappy grades, Mex?"

"Yeah," I say, closing my locker and walking over with my cleats on the cement floor.

Baileys flaming helmet is by him, and he's pulling on his custom gloves.

"Sorry to take your spot, Mex, but with the kind of games I've been having, grades aren't going to save you. No hitters are hard to come by, and you can pour all the Cokes you want all over me, but you ain't going to put out my fire, Mex."

He's wiping his Oakleys and standing up. I nod and say.

"Yeah. You're right."

"Even had to take your girl, Mex, but that comes with the territory, don't it? When you the man, you get all the goodies."

"Yeah," I say. "The same territory that comes with a steroids coke head."

Bailey's eyes become cool, and his grin is not so cocky all of a sudden. His eyes close down and then he laughs, but it is not real.

"Don't know what you're talking about, Mex."

I nod slowly and stand close to him.

"Talking about ninety-five mile an hour fastball. What do you pitch without steroids and blow, like seventy five?"

Bailey laughs and shakes head.

"That's good, man. You are creative, Mex. But just because I wiped you out with my fast ball don't give you the right to accuse me of taking steroids. But since it's your first day back, Mex, I'll overlook it."

Bailey starts walking toward the field door with his cleats clicking away.

"Coach won't overlook it," I call after him.

"Keep talking shit, Mex," he calls back.

"Raoul Sanchez won't overlook it either," I shout.

Bailey stops with his back to me. Just stops dead and turns around. That Texas grin is frozen as he comes back and stands up close. He lowers his voice and looks around like someone is hiding nearby.

"What did you say, Mex?"

"I said Raoul Sanchez is a friend of mine, and we *Mex* stick together, bro."

Bailey is sweating. Just pore-popping pearls all over. He moves his head one way and then the other. He would take a punch if he wasn't so freaked out.

"What are you saying?"

But he has lost his punch. He has lost it all. And unlike Babe Ruth, he doesn't have one last homer left in him.

"What I am saying is you're leaving the team and going back to wherever you came from...*Tex*. Because Raoul is ready to go into the coach's office and bust your ass, man. And then it's urine test time, and you ain't going to be able to drink enough water to get rid of all those 'roids. They hang around for like two weeks, man, and blow takes like a week."

Bailey swallows and shakes his head.

"I ain't leaving the team."

"Yes, you are, bro. Because if they bust you, then you can't play anywhere. So it's either you leave here, or you leave baseball for good...Tex."

Bailey's mouth hangs open. His eyes look like they are tearing up. His flaming helmet looks really stupid.

"Hey, you wouldn't do that to me, man. I mean..."

I nod slowly and grin.

"Oh, yeah. Yeah, I would, man. I'll smoke you anyway I can. Besides, we Mexs got no heart, man. It's from crossing the desert. Only the strong survive, and ain't no steroids. Just tell Coach you don't feel good and then just say you don't want to play, man. Or better, go play somewhere else. And I'll tell Raoul to be cool, and you can keep stoked on 'roids and blow."

I put on my hat and slip on my Oakleys.

"See you later....*Tex*.

38

BOB FILLER WAS SEVENTEEN-YEAR-OLD pitcher who struck out seventeen batters in the Majors. Then he went back home to finish high school. Like I went home after every practice to finish high school, and on the third day of practice Coach has an announcement. Bailey Hutchinson has transferred back to East Side School. ...Coach says he doesn't get it either, but he will be pitching for East, and we will face them in the playoffs. Coach says he's never had anybody just up and leave like that who was doing so well.

But the East coach will play anybody who will help them win, so it didn't surprise me Bailey was their pitcher. A lot of guys have gone crosstown so they could play for East. Sometimes, it's guys who didn't like the coach or guys who had trouble with grades. Or guys who quit because they don't want anyone to know they're hopped up on coke and steroids.

"Ricky, you lead off," he says, locking eyes with me.

"Great, Coach," I say.

Christine comes to my locker in the hall. She looks like a movie star. You know, all blond and tan with white teeth gnashing her gum.

She smiles and says, "Bailey left school, Ricky."

"Yeah, I heard," I say, getting out my books for class.

She is holding her books up by her chest, and I can smell her perfume.

"There goes my prom date."

"I'm sure he can still take you."

She frowns.

"You don't know anything about him leaving like that, do you?"

"Nope," I say.

Christine nods slowly and looks at me with her blue eyes turned way up. She is standing real close, and I just want to get to class. I can feel my heart, and I turn to her.

"So, are we still going to prom?"

I frown.

"Thought you were going with Bailey."

"Oh, no. I was just kidding. I was always going with you, Ricky."

I shut my locker. She goes with the wind, and somehow she knows I beat out Bailey. But that doesn't cut it anymore, and suddenly like she doesn't even seem that good looking to me now. So I shake her off and move out from my locker.

"I bet you have a lot of dudes who want to take you, Christine," I say.

She pouts with her lips pursed up.

"But I want to go with you, Ricky."

Just then I see Es walking down the hallway.

"Pardon me," I say and leave Christine and run after Es.

"Hey, Es..."

She is walking with her girls, and she turns.

"Es, can I talk to you?"

Her girls stare at me like I am trash. I get it. She makes a big show of walking over like she doesn't care and stares at me. Her eyes are suspicious.

"What do you want, Ricky?"

I shuffle my feet and pause.

"Listen, Es. I want to say I'm sorry about what I did to you before. It was wrong, and I apologize."

Her eyes go cool, and she looks at Christine.

"You mean throwing me over for Mrs. Stuck-up there."

I nod and breathe deeply.

"Yeah...Es...look...." I breathe heavy again. "I know I blew it, but will you please go to prom with me? I mean, I get it if you don't want to."

"What about her?"

I shrug.

"I had my head up my ass, you know. She is just like that Bailey dude who took my spot, lot of smoke and mirrors. I don't care about her. She doesn't mean anything to me."

Es nods slowly and lowers her eyes.

"You want to go with me over her?"

I nod. "Yeah...I do," I say, meeting her eyes.

Es wipes her eye real quickly, then nods.

"Okay. Yeah. Let's do it."

I nod and then smile.

"Cool. I'll call you."

And then Es turns back to her girls, and I watch her walk down the hall. Christine is still by my locker.

"Ricky, I waited for you while you talked to that girl. Doesn't that show I want to go with you?" she says, kind of red in the face.

"Yeah," I say, meeting those blue eyes. "Too bad I just asked her to prom, huh," I say, closing my locker.

And then I walk down the hallway, and I can feel Christine's mouth just hanging open, man. Feels good. Real good.

39

WHEN THE BLACK PLAYERS went to Cuba, they were lionized. Nobody could understand why they weren't allowed to play in the Majors in America. They went to Cuba to find the democracy they didn't have at home. Must be the way Bailey felt when he left our school, because the word is he is the starting Pitcher at East and so he must feel like he went to a different country where they still respected him.

So like, we go overtime on my homework. Mom has Econ and Math. I have Social Studies, and The Pitcher is taking a shot at English. We are like working round the clock because I have to have all this work in by the end of the week, or I don't play man and maybe not graduate. . I want to finish strong so I have to get this stuff done, but it is basically a whole semester in... one week. And my Social Studies teacher doesn't like me, and if I flunk his class, then it is game over.

Nobody is sleeping because there is no way to get it done then. I sleep and then I read. I basically have to give the origins of World War II and how the world was changed after the war. Try that one. The Pitcher is writing a conflict paper, and Mom is doing a PowerPoint presentation on the global economy and how we are all interrelated. Oh, and did I mention Biology? Yeah. I have to take a test that will determine my grade for the whole semester. I haven't even started studying for that...

But my Social Studies teacher, man, is like one of those dudes who's not too crazy about someone who's always late to his class. Yeah. That's me. Every day, just about. But you know, it's hard to get there on time, and it didn't help that he didn't like baseball. He thinks sports are for morons. He even said that once.

Mom has to ask for my assignments three times before this dude will give them up. He doesn't dig the whole IEP plan. You know, Individual Education Plan. I know he thinks I'm a slacker because I get some breaks. So he just gives me *Fs* on my papers, and then I have to redo them and he changes them to a *D*. But I need at least a *C* on this final, or I will flunk. And this dude somehow knows he is the guy with the curve, and I'm at a full count.

Not good.

And as if all this wasn't enough...I got to deal with Fernando.

But this time I have a plan. Like the Pitcher said a long time ago. It's my game, right?

40

YEAH. I KNOW. BARRY Bonds. A-Rod. Rodger Clemens. Yeah. No one could prove it, but you know they juiced. Just look at Barry Bonds before and after, man. He looks like The Terminator or Mr. America by the end. He sure doesn't look like a baseball player. And you listen to these dudes with their lawyers, and you know they did it. Just like Lance Armstrong, right. I mean, you may say, hey, these guys would have been the best anyway and everybody is doing it, but it still don't make it right.

So like, I lose no sleep over Bailey.

He had it coming, right?

And Joey says he is out to get me. He says he went psycho on Raoul, but Raoul don't play and told him to take his Texas ass back to Texas or he would send him down there in a pine box. But the word is he wants revenge, but I got other problems and one of them is Fernando. He has become even crazier, if you can believe it. Ever since he hit the Pitcher with the gun, he has been tailing me and texting me, asking for money.

But Joey says you got to make a dude like Fernando just go away. He says it's like rats; you have to make them go to someone else's house, you know. And so I started to think about a way to make Fernando go away for good, and Joey just looked at me.

"I told you, bro. I can get someone to bust a cap on him."

I said no to that. But then we sat in Joey's car in the McDonald's parking lot, and he just looks at me and grins.

"Dude. He's a con!"

I turn and look at him.

"Yeah."

"Parole officer, man. He's on parole! You can't be waving a gun around when you are on parole, man!"

So then I had my plan. I told Fernando I wanted to meet him in the parking lot behind the Target. I told him I might be able get him some of the money he wanted.

How much, he texts.

Maybe ten, I text back

Then I call the cops and say a drug deal is going to be going down in the parking lot behind the Target, and a dude will be there with a gun. Then I hang up. Like Joey said. You got to flush out the rat, man.

41

THE FIRST GREAT JEWISH baseball star was Hank Greenberg. Hard-hitting first baseman for the Detroit Lions. Up until then, a lot of Jewish players changed their names. Greenberg never considered it. The anti-Semitism of the fans and players was vicious. They called him "The Hebrew Hammer." Greenberg fought back and never backed down. He came within two runs of Babe Ruth's record of sixty homeruns in one season.

I know how Greenberg felt, man, because I can't back down now, but I just got an *F* man. That's what Mr. Ranger gave me, man, on my Social Studies paper. Mom is just staring at the Home Access grade on her computer, and her mouth is open. She had read my paper, and we had busted ass on it every night. I had explained how Hitler was on the move and started taking over countries until he got to Poland and then acted like he was going to cool out, but then took it anyway and Britain declared war on Germany, and then the Japanese attacked Pearl Harbor and we got into it.

I mean, I spent a lot of time, and Mom did, too, so I knew what was coming. Mom comes out in her low cut dress, dangling earrings and heels and tells me to come on, and it's like we are going to see the Pitcher for the first time. We caught Mr. Ranger in his class, and he looks up. He's probably in his thirties with those barbwired tats and a goatee. He's kind of a young talking teacher, and he rides a Harley.

"Mr. Ranger?" Mom says, sitting down in front of him.

He looks up, and you can see he's shocked to have this Latino mom there. I mean, we haven't slept because we have been fighting it out with every class, and I could just fall asleep right there.

"I 'm Mrs. Hernandez. Ricky's mother. I see you gave my son an *F* on his paper," she says.

Mr. Ranger's mouth kind of hangs open, and he looks down at the paper.

"That's right," he says with this Southern drawl. "Ricky did not follow directions and footnote properly."

Mom stares at him, and her chin starts moving.

"What about what he wrote?"

Mr. Ranger frowns.

"Well, I think what he wrote is fine, Mrs. Hernandez, but this class is about learning to follow instructions. Your son seems to have trouble with, that as he has trouble with being on time."

Mom leans in close with her eyes leading.

"You know if you give him an *F,* he won't pass," Mom says, sitting back, her head starting to bob.

Mr. Ranger tries for his fake smile.

"Mrs. Hernandez, I am sorry to hear that, but your son has to follow directions."

"He has an Individual Education Plan. Where are the special considerations?" Mom asks.

My teacher leans back and opens his hand.

"I have given Ricky special consideration. I'm sorry, but at some point he has to follow the rules."

Mom's mouth comes together, and her eyes move to me.

"Ricky, could you step outside for a moment?"

I stand up and go outside in the hallway but leave the door open part way. I see Mom put papers up on his desk, and she starts smiling and talking. She leans way over his desk, and Mr. Ranger eyes are on fire as Mom points down to the paper. Then she sits back and smiles, and I notice her hair is curled and she has on her makeup. She laughs and Mr. Ranger laughs.

Then their voices get quiet for a long time. Then I hear some more laughter, and ten minutes later, Mom walks out and nods to me. We start down the hallway, and I notice then Mom is kind of jiggling all over. She puts on her sunglasses when we hit the outside.

"You got a C," she says.

42

THE WAY THEY PAID off the Black Sox in Chicago was they left the money on the hotel bed. Like ten grand in an envelope. The players left their hotel room, and when they came back, the money was there. I'm in the parking lot behind Target, feeling like those guys. They must have been nervous when they agreed to take the money, the same way I 'm nervous because Fernando has just pulled up. He has come for his money, and I don't see any cops anywhere. This could go real bad if they don't show.

But I wait in Mom's van as Fernando turns off his lights and sits there a minute, then lights a cigarette and gets out. He has his shades on even though it is dark. I get out and stand in front of the van and look around again for the cops. I don't see anyone. My heart is whamming in my chest. But it's my game, and I got to take care of Fernando once and for all, or this rat will never go away. I can't have him beating up Mom or attacking the Pitcher or trying to extort money.

He stops in front of me with this big loose shirt on, and I hope his piece in his belt

"Alright, bro...you got something for me."

I nod with my mouth real dry and my heart pumping away.

"Yeah," I say

"Good, 'cuz I need the cash man," he says.

My heart is thumping so hard, I figure he can hear it. I look down and then right at him.

"Yeah, here is what I have for you," I say. "A whole lot of nothing. And that is all you are ever going to get from me and Mom...*nothing*. "

Fernando just pulls on his cigarette and looks at me.

"What, are you messing with me?"

I stare at him.

"No, I'm telling you that you don't deserve anything. All you ever did is steal from Mom and beat her and hit me, and we don't need your sorry ass coming around anymore," I say shakily.

I mean, the whole inside of me is jumping.

"So you got no money for me?"

I shake my head with my legs trembling.

"No. You will never get any money from me. Even if I get a contract for a million bucks, you won't get a cent. You don't deserve anything."

I'm looking around thinking *where are the cops where are the cops* because Fernando is pissed now. He drops his cigarette to the ground and looks up slowly, then takes off his glasses. His eyes are like bloody dark pools.

"And if you come around again, I will kick your ass," I say, trying to keep my voice steady.

His eyes grow, and then he reaches around behind him and rushes me with the gun barrel jammed against my forehead, pinning me against the van. I can smell the weed on his breath as he screams.

"You little shit, I'm gonna bust a cap in you.""

And my heart just stops and I open my mouth, because I feel like I'm going to puke when the world explodes into blue and red swirls and sirens come out of everywhere and there are cops with their guns drawn all around us.

"*Freeze, freeze!*"

Fernando's eyes go from me to the five cops who have guns pointed at us. He doesn't move, and I still have that barrel against my forehead.

"*Drop the gun! NOW!*"

I'm still against the car, and I look Fernando in the eye. We are lit up as he drops the gun and raises his hand. I raise my hands, too, and we are facing each other. I look into his eyes and nod.

"Game over, bro," I say.

43

HEY, MR. ANDERSON,

You wanted me to write something about our family; well, here it is. Like I don't know what makes someone a good citizen or a good family, but my family is for real. The Pitcher is like my dad. He's not my dad, but he wrote a paper for high school for me, besides teaching me how to pitch. He was a World Series pitcher, you know, and my Mom asked him to teach me to pitch so I could make the high school team. And then he paid for my Mom so she could go to a doctor, and then he asked her to marry him. My real dad Fernando is a real bad ass. He always beat Mom and stole our money. He is still an asshole, but is headed back to prison right now. Mom is doing my Econ and my math for me while I work on Social Studies, and the Pitcher is writing a paper for English. You may think everyone is doing my work for me, but like I'm dyslexic and not so good in school, and if they didn't help me, I can't play ball on the school team, and I probably won't graduate. Let me put it this way; my Mom is the reason I am even in school and the reason my life didn't go down the toilet with Fernando. She always made sure my clothes were clean and I had what I needed even though we were poor.

And even though she and the Pitcher hooked up, she doesn't take anything for granted. She is still always trying to save a buck, and she has only one kidney because she has lupus, and the Pitcher, he ain't doing so good either. I think he might have cancer, because he hacks blood but hasn't gone to the doctor. And me, I just lost my starting position on the baseball team and just got it back after the Pitcher showed me a new pitch. The dude that took my spot is one of those Tea Party guys who doesn't dig immigration or Mexicans. And one reason Mom lost her job at Target, which was a long time ago, was because she was trying to make people aware of how we need to reform our laws on that.

So now I got to go play in the playoffs against this dude who is on steroids and pitches like ninety five, but the Pitcher says you got to outthink him, and Mom's dream for me is to graduate and go to college, and mine is to play for the Cubs, so I'm not sure what is going to happen there, but I gotta get my social studies done. Like I said, I don't know what makes a family, but we all pick each other up, you know, when we are down and I think that makes a us a good family, and to send my Mom back to Mexico would really break us apart, so I guess I'm asking you to let her stay.

Because if she goes, I'm going, and the Pitcher will go, too. Because we are family, man.

Sincerely,

Ricky Hernandez

44

THE THING IS, WITH baseball, you need all nine players. You can be the best pitcher in the world, but you need the other guys to win. So that's how it is with family, too. You need everyone to go in there and win. Mom helps me get ready for prom .....and the Pitcher takes all these shots in the driveway. Es and I go to prom, and it's pretty cool. If you look at our picture, man, then you know we are having a good time. We rode in a limousine that the Pitcher paid for. Pretty cool, bro. And then we danced, and that's like when I saw Baily and Christine.

I didn't think that dude could come to our prom, but there he was and they are like on the dance floor, and suddenly we are all dancing next to each other. He and Christine are like almost on top of each other, and then they start making out. Es looks great in this light blue dress, and I'm happening in my tuxedo, and I'm trying to maneuver away from them, but that's when Bailey lets fly, you know.

"Hey...maybe you can swat at that disco ball, Mex," he says over Christine's shoulder.

I ignore him because our game is tomorrow, and I know his play.

"You know, just pretend it's a piñata, and your Mex girl can have at it," he continues.

Es. She don't play. She is suddenly off me and goes over and kicks that Bailey dude right in his ass. I mean square, man, and he kind of lifts up and whips around. He is in like this black and white get up, and his face turns red.

"You crazy Mexican bitch!" he shouts.

Es, she gets right up in his face.

"Yeah, I am going to kick your racist Texas ass again," she shouts.

And then Christine is glaring at her.

"Forget her, she is just low class," she says.

Es is going after her and gets right in her face.

"Who are you calling low class, Miss Stuck-up Bitch!"

Bailey is kind of freaking now.

"Mex, get your Chiquita out of here, man, before I forget I'm a gentleman."

"Go on, bitch, and I'll kick your skinny ass next," Es says, moving on him, and he backs up.

You don't want a Mexican chick mad at you, man. Believe me.

Christine isn't moving, because Es is all over her shit.

"Come on, Es, let's get out of here," I say, pulling her back.

Christine is all red faced, and Bailey nods to me.

"I'll kick your ass tomorrow, Mex," he says.

"Better double up on your 'roids then," I reply.

Bailey looks like he wants to go at it, but Christine has taken off and he goes after her. We go outside where it's cool and the stars are bright in the parking lot. Es is lighting up a cigarette and shaking her head.

"I should have kicked that bitch in her ass."

I had to grin, seeing Bailey's face again.

"Well, you kicked his ass."

Es smiles, and then we both laugh and lean against the parking lot fence. I borrow a cigarette, and we smoke together.

"You going to college?" she asks suddenly.

I shrug and inhale the smoke.

"I don't know. I just am trying to graduate, you know. Don't know if my grades are good enough for college."

Es has sparkles in her hair and on her lips and eyes.

"You going, Es?"

She shakes her head.

"Nah, got to work for my mother in the salon."

I nod slowly.

"Yeah, well, I thought I was going to play baseball, but I don't know now."

Es turns then and looks at me the way Joey did.

"You going to play, Ricky Hernandez. That is one thing I know. "

"Oh, yeah?"

Es holds her cigarette low and looks at me.

"You got it going on. I can tell. "

I smile and feel really good that I didn't take Christine to prom.

"Thanks, Es."

"I always knew it. Something about you. I'm going to say I went to prom with Ricky Hernandez one day."

I looked at her, and then we kissed, you know. Like a long, long time.

45

JOE DIMAGGIO GOT A hit for fifty-six consecutive games. No one has ever come near that record since. People couldn't believe it when it was happening. And they say it will never happen again. I dunno. You gotta have hope, you know. That's why I'm not sweating it, man. Bailey is pitching for East, and we are in the first game of the playoffs. The newspapers are calling it a blood feud. Sports writers love guys like Bailey and me because we really do hate each other, and since he ended up at East, we are facing off in the first round of the playoffs.

And it is beautiful, man. No wind. Bright sunshine. The world is in place, and Jigger Hix is in the stands along with Mom, the Pitcher, Es, and Joey and his homeboys with their shaved heads and goatees. Joey holds up a bottle of pills to Bailey and yells.

"Yo, you want some more 'roids and some blow, man?"

Bailey just stares at him. Then Jigger comes over to the fence and tells me he was here to watch Bailey and me face off.

"Wouldn't miss it for the world," he says palming a cigar.

And yeah, I'm nervous, but it had to have happened sooner or later. Bailey is nailing the catcher's glove with rifle shots. *Crack. Crack. Crack.* Seems like he is pitching one hundred miles an hour, and he looks juiced. His eyes are big, and he stares at me like he wants to kill me. Same way Fernando did when they took him away in the squad car and Mom got off the phone and I didn't have to press charges for attempted murder, because he violated his parole anyway with the gun.

"What did you say to him to get him so mad?" Mom wants to know

I shrug. "I just told him I wasn't going to give him any money."

Mom nods. "And you set up that meeting?"

"Uh-huh."

"Well, he is going back to prison for violating his parole," Mom says.

"Guess some things just work out," I say.

And now I'm going up to bat, and it is time, you know. I walk up to the batter's box, and Bailey is grinning and mouths MEX and eyes me like someone about to shoot someone. I take some practice swings, and I see Jigger Hix watching by the fence. Does it get any more real than right now? All I can do is remember what the Pitcher said the day before.

We had been working on the forkball. Think of a meteorite that nobody knows where it will land. That's the forkball. It feels like my arm is going to tear off every time I throw it, but I want that pitch. It has Bailey written all over it. The Pitcher, he's hacking blood now that's bright red on the grass. He spits when he thinks I'm not looking, but I see it.

"My game is all mine," he says when I tell him again he should go to the doctor.

"I been prodded and poked my whole life. I'm done with all that," he says.

And then we are sitting on the bench enjoying the breeze, and he tells me about how poor he was in Arkansas and how he only had the rocks to throw. I had heard the story before, but I always liked to listen to it again. Ball players were mostly all poor then. They always had different jobs. The Pitcher had a donut shop for a while and then a bar. Then he had a motorcycle shop.

"You had to because they didn't pay enough then," he says.

And then we just sat there. I told him he got a C on his paper about hitting a Home Run in the World Series. My teacher Ms.

Zimmer said it wasn't believable and that it was obvious I didn't know what hitting a homerun was like. The Pitcher shook his head when I told him that. But now he is hacking like his lungs are coming up. And I know this is not good, and Mom is going crazy because he won't go see a doctor.

The Pitcher crosses his legs and looks across the field.

"I'll make you a deal. You get a homerun and strike out this Bailey kid in the playoff, and then I'll go to the doctor."

"So you're not going to go," I say, looking at him.

He frowns.

"Where's your goddamn confidence?" he says.

I take the deal, but I don't feel so good about it right now. I walk into the batter's box, and in comes the fastballs like bullets. I swing, but there is only air. I am behind. *Strike one. Strike Two.* Then I catch his fastball for a deep one in center field. It's gone. I know it is, and I begin tearing up the bases, but the centerfielder makes one of those plays no one can believe and leans over the fence and turns a homer into an out. I stop on second base as Bailey grins and guns his finger at me. I feel like he just shot me because I see the Pitcher by the fence looking pale. He spits, and I don't want to think about that blood in the dirt.

46

TED WILLIAMS HIT LIKE Babe Ruth and Lou Gehrig, but he wasn't loved. Once after the fans had booed him, he vowed never to tip his hat again after a homerun. He didn't feel he owed the fans anything but hits. He never did either. When you are up, the fans love you, but when you are losing, nobody wants to know you. Like with me right now. It ain't going good, man. I have loaded them up in the ninth, and Bailey is up. He's got me for a double and a single, and my fastball is out of gas. We are up by one, but if Bailey gets anything, then we are in trouble.

Bailey is eyeing me and swinging like a wild man. He slams the bat against the plate, and I come back and give him a curve and sinker, and he fouls off. Then he protects, and I rack up three balls pinching the corners. And so we are at full count.

The whole world is a full count against you, right? But you know, you really do have a responsibility to your talent, man, whatever it is and whatever it takes, and the Pitcher is holding up his hands like a peace sign. Yeah. *Forkball*. Time to go for it. People are standing up, and I can see Jigger Hix, and then I see Es and Mom and the Pitcher. Everybody wants to see what's going to happen. Bailey is there with his flames on his helmet and his Texas mouth and his blue eyes, and I can see Eric and his boys, and Christine is there and, you know, the whole quilt of my life.

And it is time for the Pitcher to go see a doctor, and it is time for me to go play baseball. And it is time for me to graduate. So that's why you pitch, you know. Because it is what you do. And all the rocks I've thrown and all the times Fernando has hit me and threatened us and all the times people get over on us because we are Mexicans. And maybe the dude is reading my essay and maybe he's thinking that people who dream should be in this country, right? Because, I mean, that is what America is about. Dreams, man. Right? Dreamers and dreams. And I am a dream kid, and here comes my dream kid pitch.

And Bailey, he has dreams, too, but he doesn't play fair. And so here comes the perfect pitch. I pull in and split my fingers on the ball and shove it way down in my palm and kick back and come over the top and jerk down at the last minute, and that weird-ass knuckle ball fast ball starts its journey the way Mom started hers all those years ago when she came here with her dream. She decided my dream was hers, and still that ball is rolling straight along just like me slipping on that graduation gown man that is so slippery and blue and I am walking into the stands at high school with all those other people and that tune is playing and it is kind of sad, you know, because it means something is ending.

And it hits me, as that forkball starts to do its thing, that seventeen years is pretty quick. That Mom and I will go apart now. We have been together all this time, and now something is ending, and we are all lining up in the stadium, man, as *Pomp and Circumstance* rolls out, because Mom got me through Biology, Econ, Math, Social Studies, and the Pitcher kicked it in for English. Now that that ball is starting to wobble and weave and Bailey is trying to track it, but good luck with that because my track has never been straight, and suddenly I turn around in that stadium. Because we are lined up in our caps and gowns, and I want to see Mom.

And in that sea of blue robes I turn and look into the stadium for her. I mean, I want to see her before I can't ever see her again, and all I see is all these parents, man, when suddenly this person stands up and starts waving her hands. *"Ricky! Ricky! Ricky!"* And I wave back, and she shouts across that whole stadium, man. *"You did it, Ricky! You did it!"* And my eyes, man, just go bad and I can't see, and Mom yells again. *"I love you, Ricky!"* and then I yell back, I mean, right in the middle of the ceremony, but I don't care.

"I love you, Mom!"

And that forkball breaks down in the way God intended, man, in a way no one can ever predict, and Bailey swings for the ball that just isn't there anymore, and no steroid in the world can help, because the big dog from Texas just struck out, and me, man....*me.*

I can't talk anymore because...well....

I graduated from high school, bro.

47

OKAY. NOW THE *MONEYBALL* moment. You know the scene where the dudes slide the check. Well, maybe not exactly. We are having a party for Mom at our house. Guess my essay was pretty good, because the government dude said Mom can stay and she's on track to become a citizen. Actually, it's my graduation party, and everybody is having a great time when the doorbell rings, and there is Jigger Hix.

"I just wanted to stop by before I caught a plane back to Chicago," he explains to Mom and me and the Pitcher in the living room. "It is a real honor, sir, to meet you," he says.

He then turns to Mom.

"Is there somewhere we can all talk?"

But now we are all sitting down at the kitchen table, and Jigger Hix is looking at me, and I'm thinking he is going to like slide a check across the table like in the movie and say "This is what the Chicago Cubs think of you, Ricky." But he doesn't do that. He just puts an envelope on the table and looks around the room and says, "I want you to think real hard, Ricky, on what is in this envelope and then give me a call."

Mom looks like she is about to burst, and even the Pitcher can't take his eyes off the envelope.

Jigger, who is red faced anyway and looks like he should always have a cigar in his mouth, stands and nods around the room to everyone.

"Well, I look forward to hearing from you folks."

And then he leaves, and we are all just sitting there. Mom looks at me.

"Well, are you going to open it?"

I pause and stare at the long white envelope that holds my future. I pick it up slowly, and it feels fat. I hold it up to the light, and the Pitcher snorts. I then hold it down and take a deep breath.

"Alright," I say and thumb open the flap.

I shakily take out the letter.

And begin to read.

ACKNOWLEDGMENTS

Many thanks to John, Joe, and Leticia, who have kept the pitches coming. And to my son Clay once again for teaching me what pitching and perseverance are all about.

COMING SOON
THE PITCHER 3!